I0534248

THE BELFORE

VOID

JOEY ROGERS

THE BELFORE VOID

by

JOEY ROGERS

Copyright © 2019 GegoDyne, LLC.

www.gegodyne.com

VERSION 1.03

CHAPTER 1

THE BATTERY

THIRTY YEARS EARLIER

Jenny stared at the graph displayed on her computer screen. She hadn't taken her eyes off of it for over an hour. When the splatter of dots started to move around their axes as if they were performing a maypole dance, she leaned back and rubbed her eyes. She couldn't believe that the last four years of her life could be reduced to a single scatter plot, one page of paper. The results seemed disproportionate to the time she had invested and the student debt she had accrued. Her research had already accumulated enough data to complete her dissertation and earn her Ph.D., but she wanted to crown her achievement with a significant breakthrough. She needed something more than a "Dr." in front of her name if she wanted to guarantee her future career.

Pursuing a science degree didn't thrill Jenny's parents. They were leftover hippies who believed a physics degree was too closely related to the establishment. Its uncaring facts, constraining rules, and bureaucratic procedures didn't represent the free-spiritedness or harmony they raised their daughter to believe. But Jenny had always known what she wanted to do. Her mind wanted to take things apart and figure out how they worked. She needed to explore how the universe worked, and physics allowed her to redefine those boundaries. She also wasn't afraid of getting a student loan, so her parents didn't have much sway over her choice of major. When Jenny told them she was staying in school to get a Ph.D., they wanted to kidnap her and run away to a commune in California. She didn't get their approval until she pitched her graduate work as being green-adjacent. They understood nothing about her research, but they told everyone that their daughter was saving the world. It embarrassed her immensely. Her work might help the planet one day, but that wasn't her primary concern. She needed a way to continue her learning even after leaving the university, and she had to position herself in a career that would make that happen.

Jenny yawned and stretched her arms above her head. She had been at her workstation since before the sun came up. Spending quality time with her data was hard to do, but getting to the physics building before anyone else was the best way to make it happen. When she looked at the scatter plot graph again, something in the pattern of dots leaped off the screen. It was just like one of those stereogram posters where a hidden picture suddenly appeared amidst its randomness. Why hadn't she ever seen it before? She thought her eyes were still playing tricks on her and rubbed them again. The graph didn't change. Her keyboard sounded like a machine gun firing as she entered commands to filter out some data points and generate a new plot.

She reached for her coffee mug as she waited on the computer and sighed when she realized it was empty. She wanted to get some caffeine, but she couldn't leave the computer. When the output popped up on the screen, she couldn't believe what she saw. A trend line had been hiding in plain sight, and it increased exponentially. She had never seen it before because she wasn't looking for anything so fantastic. The data suggested that her experimental battery could store an order of magnitude more energy than she had ever considered possible.

She hoped her analysis wasn't a mistake, but it was too incredible not to share. She emailed a copy of the graph to another grad student in the program, Daniel, with a one-word subject, "Wow!" She wanted to spend more time investigating her new find, but she had to get ready for the weekly experiment.

Every Wednesday morning, Jenny used her scheduled time in the physics lab to conduct experiments on her prototype battery. Her research centered on the idea that she could tuck energy into superimposed quantum states by varying the frequency patterns of electrons racing around a ring of superconducting filaments. Most scientists labeled her nonconventional design as pseudo-science, but she had collected substantial evidence proving otherwise.

The next battery test was less than an hour away. She had been through the proposed configuration a dozen times. She had even gone over it with Daniel, who had fabricated the battery as part of his research. It, unfortunately, wasn't an ordinary Wednesday. A TV crew would be filming her work for a piece on the local news. She had tried to persuade her adviser not to put the battery on display so early in its development, but he dismissed her concerns. He also burdened her with the task of arranging the puff piece. She had cashed in a favor to make it happen, but even a minor glitch with the battery test would be humiliating and could set back her research. Broadcasting her failure to thousands could do permanent damage to her career, and that was something she wanted to avoid.

Jenny drew in a deep breath, held it for a few seconds, and reviewed the upcoming battery experiment from the beginning. She wanted to incorporate more aggressive changes into the test to see if she could push the trend line even higher, but it was too risky with the TV crew there. A well-planned test was her secret to success, and last-minute alterations were never a good idea under any circumstance. On her second pass through the test parameters, the sound of keys jingling in the hallway interrupted her analysis.

"Good morning, Jenny," Professor Jonathan Rutledge said as he strutted past her and disappeared into his office.

Jenny cringed. Nice of the person in *charge* to show up. She wished Rutledge was more interested in directing her dissertation than chasing after his precious tenure, but he was the only one in the physics department who would sponsor her research. She was simultaneously grateful to and repulsed by him.

"Coffee!" Rutledge commanded from his office.

Jenny pinched her lips together and counted to five. She debated whether to ignore him, but she didn't. She needed another cup of coffee anyway, and it was just courteous to get him one. Right? Besides, if she wanted to get this day off to a good start, fetching a cup of coffee was a trivial price to pay.

"It's about time," Rutledge said when she handed him a steaming cup. "Are we ready?"

"Daniel is in the lab prepping the equipment, and I just verified all the parameters for the next run." She offered him a printout detailing the upcoming experiment. "I also discovered a trend in the data. You should take a look at it."

"I don't care about that." He tossed the papers on the desk. "Has the media arrived?"

"Yes… sort of." She looked down, hoping to conceal the anger in her eyes.

"Explain." He set his coffee on his desk hard enough to lose a few milky drops and waited for her reply.

"It's a local TV crew, but they're an affiliate of a major network." Her tone was as upbeat as it could be without exaggerating their importance.

Rutledge's face hardened. "I expected more than the J-school flunkies who lacked the ambition to leave the two-bit town of Belfore."

Jenny wanted to dump her coffee on his head, but she knew that would get her kicked out of the program. He would then claim all of her work instead of the majority. She wouldn't let that happen, but he wasn't going to diminish all of her extra work either. "I had to pull a lot of strings to get those *J-school flunkies* to even do a segment on the battery.

Besides, if the test is successful, the national news will pick up the story."

"They'd better." He snorted and scanned through the first couple of pages of her report before losing interest.

Daniel knocked on the doorframe and poked his head in the office. "Dr. Rutledge, everything's ready in the lab."

"We'll be right there, Daniel," he replied with a sharp tone. "Arrange all of my protocol sheets and don't omit my talking points this time."

"Yes, sir." The assistant turned to leave.

"And make sure you prime the coil before I get there. I don't want my presentation to suffer while we're all waiting around on you."

"Yes, sir," Daniel said again and dashed out of the office.

Jenny waited until the sound of his footsteps faded. "Weren't you a little hard on him?"

Rutledge rolled his eyes. "If he did what I told him, I would already have my tenure."

Jenny started to say something but stopped. She liked Daniel—he was a lot smarter than Rutledge—but she didn't like him enough to make waves. She also didn't want the news crew to record one of the famous Rutledge meltdowns for posterity and have it associated with her battery. Daniel would have to take one for the team.

Rutledge took a final sip of coffee, got up, and swaggered over to the wall where a dozen lab coats hung on small hooks. He ran his hand through the collection as he narrowed down the candidates. There were several colors and styles, but he stopped on a knee-length, white coat.

"Stereotypical rather than stylish," he said, holding up his selection. He removed his sports jacket and straightened his maroon and blue tie, the school colors, before slipping on the slim-fit coat. A full-length mirror hung next to the lab coats, and he stared at his reflection a little too long before combing his fingers through his hair.

With the TV crew there, Jenny thought he should be more worried about the experiment than how his hair looked. But what would she know? She was just the lowly grad student who did all of his work.

"I believe everything is ready now," Rutledge said. "We should go to the lab."

CHAPTER 2

THE DISCOVERY

Belfore University's physics lab provided an environment to conduct a variety of experiments, and Jenny had a permanent station set up there to support her battery research. With a half-dozen tables topped with a thick layer of black soapstone and a variety of test equipment, the work area was small. The addition of a cameraman, a sound man, and a local news producer made the room cramped.

Rutledge grimaced as soon as he entered the lab. "They're too close to the coil."

Daniel ran over to reposition the crew.

The induction coil was a solid torus. It could have been mistaken for the inner tube from a fat bicycle tire, only it was a solid piece of metal weighing a hundred pounds. The inside diameter was fifteen inches, and the device stood upright on one of the lab tables. It looked like it was ready to roll away except for several heavy gauge electrical cables attached to its base.

The television producer made his way over to Rutledge. Despite his youth, his hair was thinning. He was overweight and wore a cheap, wrinkled suit. Rutledge glared down at the man. "Can I help you?"

"I'm Jason Reed, the person in charge of shooting this piece." He reached out to shake hands, but Rutledge didn't reciprocate. "We'll set up in front of that big metal donut, and I'll ask you a few questions."

Rutledge winced. "It's a very advanced piece of—"

The producer held up his hand to stop the speech. "I don't do the science, Dr. Rutledge. That's your job."

"Surely, you will not be on camera with me," Rutledge's said.

"We just shoot you and splice in questions from the reporter *du jour*."

"Why isn't a real reporter here?"

The producer shook his head. "That's not how this works." He looked back at his crew and made a twirling motion with his finger, and a red light illuminated on the camera. A lanky soundman thrust a boom tipped with a fluffy microphone toward a point above the two men's heads. Rutledge flinched.

The producer pointed at his own face. "Look at me when you answer, not the camera."

Rutledge was a practiced performer—if nothing else—and his face transformed from a vibrating snarl to an intellectual smile.

The producer clapped his hands together. "Belfore University, Battery Experiment." He pulled an index card out of his shirt pocket and moved to a position outside the camera's view. Rutledge looked directly at the camera until the producer cleared his throat and made a V-sign with his fingers and directed the professor to look at him. "Tell us why we're here today?"

"We're testing my quantum stacking hypothesis to see if we can push fifty-kilowatt hours into the induction coil you see behind me."

The producer shook his head. "You need to dumb it down. Let's try that again."

Rutledge paused a second, recomposed himself, and started over. "We're trying to increase the amount of energy we can store in a revolutionary battery I created here as part of my research."

The producer nodded. "Why is the battery special?"

"I'm using a new, low-cost, high-temperature superconducting material to store electricity in a radically different way."

"Why is that better?"

"If the battery proves itself—as I hope it does here today—there will be a giant leap in energy storage technology. Chemical batteries will become obsolete. These new power packs will be smaller, provide instantaneous charging, and have double or triple the capacity."

"What are the applications of this technology?"

"Electric vehicles, primarily, but any large-scale use of battery power is fair game."

"It's the late '90s, and electric vehicles have all been failures. Why go after that sector?"

"My technology will make them viable and virtually eliminate environmental concerns."

"We don't usually report on a battery test. Why has your research garnered so much attention?"

"As I said, I'm implementing a new approach to storing electricity. The torus, the ring"—Rutledge pointed back at the device—"contains miles of braided, superconducting filaments that create a quantum effect through magnetic flux compression. My battery stores, or stacks, energy more efficiently than conventional technologies."

The producer waved his index card in the air. "I won't be able to use that, Doctor. You're going way over everyone's head. Just tell us about the fancy light show."

Rutledge paused for a second. "We don't fully understand why, but charging the coil produces an interesting visual phenomenon. I'm calling it the Rutledge effect."

"I've heard that it's quite spectacular. Can you describe it?"

"Yes, it's delightful but not the focus of this test. I'm trying to revolutionize the way we store energy, not create a light show."

"Without the light show, Doctor, nobody would be interested in your battery." Jason glanced at Jenny.

Rutledge's cool facade wavered for a second. He deserved respect for his serious research, and he wouldn't win addition funding or get tenure with a stupid light show. But he needed the publicity. "I speculate that the quantum effect excites the air molecules occupying the center of the ring, creating an unusual effect. It's like the ionized gas in a neon light bulb. The colored lights swirl around as the coil charges and remain visible until the energy dissipates."

"Will we be seeing the light show today?"

"Yes," Rutledge said with no elaboration.

The producer made a throat-cutting motion with his hand, and the camera's red light blinked off, and the microphone retracted.

Rutledge strode over to Jenny at her control console. "This... kid is unacceptable. How dare he insult me like that?"

"I don't think Jason was insulting you," she said in a reassuring tone. "It's just that experimental battery tests aren't very entertaining or newsworthy. I had to sell him the idea of how incredible the light show is just to get him to come. And it's our best chance of getting the battery on the national news if that's really what you want to do."

"It better." His lips twisted as he tried to compose himself.

"All preflight checks are green," she said. "We're ready to go." She continued to enter commands, and a series of blue lights illuminated around the surface of the metal ring.

Daniel grabbed a handful of safety glasses out of a cabinet and distributed them to everyone in the lab.

The producer twirled his finger in the air again, and the camera light blinked on.

"Put your protective eyewear on," Rutledge said and waited for everyone to comply. "Energize the induction coil."

Jenny toggled several switches, each making a loud clunk. "Increasing to Level One," she said and turned a large dial on her console. An electrical hum filled the room, but nothing else seemed to change.

"Increase to Level Two," Rutledge said. The hum got louder, and the lights dimmed for a second.

"The secondary transformer has engaged," Jenny said.

"Increase to Level Three." He turned to face the camera. "This is what we're calling the Rutledge effect," he said with obvious pride.

Jenny counted down. "Three... two... one."

A shimmering light filled the open center of the ring, and swaths of pastel colors swirled around, creating a hypnotic effect. The soundman dropped the microphone into the shot nearly hitting Rutledge. The cameraman looked up from his viewfinder to verify that he didn't see video artifacts, and the producer forgot to ask the next question.

Rutledge didn't wait for the amateur crew to regain their competence and continued on his own. "At this point, we can disconnect the coil from external power and extract enough electricity from it to drive an electric vehicle for fifty miles. That's the most energy we've been able to store in our laboratory experiments, but it's only slightly better than existing technologies." He made a dramatic pause. "Now for the real test." He nodded to Jenny. "Increase to Level Four."

Jenny froze.

Rutledge turned away from the camera and gave Jenny a look that conveyed the jeopardy her position was in if she didn't comply.

After a tense moment, Jenny said, "Increasing to Level Four."

The lights dimmed again, and the swirling colors in the center of the ring became brighter and moved faster. Rutledge looked back at the readouts on Jenny's console and did some calculations in his head. He turned to the camera but remembered to look at the producer. "We've just doubled an electric vehicle's range to one hundred miles and broken the world record for energy density." The hum grew louder as electricity continued to flow into the coil. "The range has double again to two hundred miles. Now three hundred miles, and it's still increasing." Over the roaring hum, Rutledge shouted, "I've done it!"

Daniel clapped his hands above his head in triumph, and Jenny smiled cautiously. But their moment of celebration was short-lived. A blinding flash forced everyone to close their eyes, and a loud bang shook the lab. The center of the ring transformed from a whimsical flurry of lights to a jet-black hole sucking the air out of the room. Everyone's ears popped, and the door to the hallway burst open, feeding the ring with even more air.

Rutledge's lab coat flapped in the airflow until it inflated like a parachute. He tried to grip the edge of the lab table as he strained against the drag, but he was slipping toward the vortex. His safety glasses flew off and disappeared, and sheer terror replaced his usual arrogant expression.

The soundman struggled to hang onto to his boom until losing his balance. He struck his head on the corner of a lab table as he tumbled to the floor. He left a bright trail of blood as he slid toward the ring. Daniel grabbed the unconscious man's foot and clung to a table leg so tightly, his knuckles turned white.

The cameraman was the closest to the door, and he dropped his equipment and crouched down as he clomped toward the exit. The producer caught the camera as it flew by. He wouldn't miss an opportunity to record the disaster happening around him and panned the camera to capture what appeared to be the inside of a tornado. He underestimated the force of the turbulence and fell to the floor, but he didn't let go of the camera.

Daniel braced himself and stretched out a leg for the producer to grasp, and the human chain they formed stretched until he screamed. He was about to let go when the ring sucked both Rutledge and Jenny through the opening it created. Their bodies blocked the airflow long enough for Daniel and the producer to drag the soundman into the hallway.

After a hundred and forty-two seconds, the black hole in the center of the ring disappeared.

Jenny was a minor footnote in the discovery of what became known as the Void. Rutledge turned into a scientific martyr, one who died pursuing research that would change the world. It didn't matter that the portal he created was an accident or that many questioned his role in the technology's creation. It didn't matter that Belfore University was a second-rate college in a backward state. The Belfore Void sparked the most colossal research endeavor ever conceived and framed a new scientific discipline—Voidology. It was a new Moon shot, a great challenge humanity couldn't get enough of.

Daniel and the television crew survived their harrowing brush with the Void. So did the video footage of its discovery, which played on television more than the Apollo 11 Moon landing. Yet, unlike Rutledge, who became a posthumous cult figure, no lasting fame attached itself to the survivors.

CHAPTER 3

THE EXHIBITION

PRESENT DAY

Andi glanced at her watch. It was almost time to start the weekly exhibition, Introduction to the Void, and she was ready to get it over with. She believed her new responsibility as a presenter was some form of karmic revenge, but she wasn't quite sure what she had done to deserve it.

She fidgeted with the mic on her headset, trying to get it in the right position. "Please take a seat. We'll get started shortly."

The speakers reverberated her announcement until she toggled the transmitter off and on. She didn't have a soundman, even though she had asked for one, and had to perform a mandatory reboot every time she used the outdated equipment. If something as simple as a microphone had problems, she had no idea how any of the other equipment in the physics building managed to work.

A group of twenty entered the auditorium and started taking seats in the back row. Andi waved at them and pointed to a strip of empty seats near the front. There was plenty of room, and they needed to be able to see her performance. She smiled as they approached until a cloud of what smelled like straight bourbon wafted over her, and their volume increased to the point where she could make out everything they were saying. She frowned but only on the inside.

It was two minutes past the starting time, and Andi gave up on any late arrivals. She signaled for the doors to be closed. The house lights dimmed, and an usher bounded down the center aisle. He handed her a tally counter, then disappeared into the wings. She frowned, on the outside this time, when she read seventy-eight. The attendance had been worse, but if she had to put on a performance, she wanted an adequate audience for the five-hundred-seat auditorium.

A spotlight snapped on, prompting Andi to move into position behind the lectern. It was too tall for her, and she had to stand on her tiptoes to make it work. She had also requested a light man, so she could have a more dynamic presentation, but an usher flipping a switch was all she got. She tapped on her microphone to make sure it was still working and broadcasted a big smile across the entire audience.

"Hello, everyone!" she said. "My name is Andalusia, but everyone calls me Andi. I'm a doctoral student here at Belfore University." Staying in the beam of light, she moved to the front of the lectern to make her presentation more personable and to make the lectern's improper height less of an issue. Public speaking was nothing for her. She was an actor, after all, and the only one in the Voidology program capable of standing in front of an audience without freezing up or blabbering like an idiot.

"How many of you are from out-of-state?"

Half of the audience raised a hand.

"How many from outside the United States?"

A dozen hands went up.

"How many alumni?"

The raucous group down in front all waved their hands. "Go Bulls!" one of them yelled, and the audience laughed, which encouraged them to make even more noise.

Andi shouted the school's rallying cry, "Horns up!" She made a gesture with her fingers that resembled the horns of a bull and then raised her arms into a touchdown signal.

The alumni group clapped and hooted.

"Thank you all for coming to this week's exhibition." Andi looked around the large room at the clusters of people in the audience. "This year marks the thirtieth anniversary of the Void's discovery." She clapped, and the audience did too. "Who's seen a portal opening on TV?"

Everyone's hand raised. The portal discovery video was mandatory viewing in every grade that taught a science class, and the footage was the most viewed video on YouTube, ever.

"Wonderful!" She paused and then said, "How many of you have witnessed an opening in person?"

Nobody lifted their hand.

"Really?" She lifted a single eyebrow. "You're going to be in for a treat."

She twirled around and raised her hand to direct everyone's attention toward the maroon and blue stage curtains behind her. The lights faded, and she carefully made her way off the stage in the darkness.

An expectant buzz filled the auditorium as the curtains mechanically rose into the fly. The audience couldn't see the transition in the darkness, and there were audible gasps when a circular glow appeared with arcs of electricity shooting out in all directions. A light behind the one-meter ring slowly illuminated until the device was fully visible to the audience. The mini-lightning bolts faded away. They were fake, just a computer-generated image projected onto the ring's surface from the ceiling. It supposedly added drama to the presentation, but Andi thought it was pathetic for them to use such a cheap trick. She had asked to have it taken out, but there it was.

"You're looking at a Rutledge Mark V Induction Coil," she said into her microphone from offstage. "It's currently charging and will create a portal opening to the Void after accumulating enough energy."

The crowd was silent, mesmerized by the object. They all knew what to expect, even if they hadn't seen it in person.

"The induction coil is behind a one-foot-thick acrylic barrier laced with lead. It's both transparent and capable of absorbing any radiation emitted from an open portal."

The electrical hum grew louder.

"A portal is like a doorway into outer space, and opening it will cause explosive decompression, just as it did when Dr. Jonathan Rutledge created the first portal and lost his life in the process."

A substantial amount of electricity coursed through the high-voltage equipment, charging the induction coil. The effect was a low-frequency rumble that vibrated the seats in the auditorium like a minor earthquake. Before it reached its crescendo, a shriek came from the audience.

"There's nothing to fear," Andi reassured them in her best stage voice. "The sound you're feeling is a perfectly normal part of the charging process. All the air inside the test chamber was pumped out, so there will be no explosive decompression when the portal opens. Just relax and enjoy the show." She felt like she was operating a ride at Disney World full of nervous children. Please keep your hands and arms inside the ride at all times, and hang on to your personal belongings.

Bright colors appeared in the center of the ring and started spinning inside the open space. The vibrant hues performed a frenetic dance, capturing the entire audience's attention.

"The colorful lights you see result from quantum fluctuations. It's a unique property of the induction coil, and it's called the Rutledge effect after its late discoverer."

The center of the ring became more active, and a group of kids squealed with excitement as the light show amped up. The neon-colored lights grew brighter and projected erratic patterns onto the walls of the auditorium. It was unlike any special effect Hollywood could manufacture, and a camera couldn't capture the depth of the experience.

"Like I said, it's spectacular," Andi said. She thought it looked like a flashy toilet flushing, but she had seen it a dozen times.

When the light show had illuminated the entire auditorium, Andi walked back out onto the stage. She pointed at the ring behind the transparent barrier. "This one-meter ring is the largest Rutledge induction coil in the world and opens the largest portal ever created."

The vibrations became more profound, and the Rutledge effect intensified.

Andi glanced at her watch and waited a couple of seconds. "Here we go," she said and closed her eyes.

A bright flash filled the auditorium like a hundred flashbulbs going off simultaneously. The hum stopped, and the light show vanished. The ring appeared completely inactive, except the hole in its center had turned black.

"While the induction coil appears to be inoperative, the center of the ring is actually a portal, a doorway, to another place. I would like to be more specific, but even after decades of research, we still don't know exactly where the portal leads. It could be to a sub-space pocket, another dimension, or even another universe." She slowly shook her head. "But we don't know where it goes... yet." She ended with an optimistic inflection.

Andi knew she was a good actor. She had to be because she didn't believe anything associated with the Void was worthwhile. After thirty years of failure, teasing the audience that something useful would come from it was a lie. It also meant that her job as the DJ to a glorified disco was a complete waste of her time.

But she had made a deal with her father...

On the left side of the test chamber, there was movement and sounds of whirring articulation. A multi-jointed, robotic arm moved into view and reached down to grasp a three-meter-long pole resting horizontally on a stand. The mechanical hand effortlessly lifted the pole along with a spherical payload mounted on its tip.

"Today's exhibition will insert a test package filled with experiments through the portal and remain there for almost two minutes." Andi looked back at the ring and then to the audience and grinned. "Now, it's time for the magic to begin."

The platform supporting the ring rotated ninety degrees. Only a profile view of the ring was visible to the audience, and they watched the robotic arm insert the payload through the center of the ring and disappear. The audience gasped.

"As you may have noticed, the test package did not emerge from the other side of the induction coil. It's in what we call the Void, the place on the other side of the portal."

The mechanical arm pushed the pole into the Void until only a few inches remained visible. As Andi had forewarned, it looked like a magic trick, one that could have been performed with mirrors, but it wasn't. It was real.

After two minutes, the robotic arm began moving again and extracted the pole from the Void along with its payload. The ring rotated back to face the audience, and everyone gazed into the blackness filling its center. There was another flash, and the audience could see through the center of the ring to the wall behind it.

The portal was closed, and the ring was once again an inert piece of gray metal.

"Every portal to the Void closes after 142 seconds," Andi said over a loud hissing noise. "You're hearing the air being pumped back into the test chamber. When it's back to one atmosphere, the other grad students will retrieve the payload."

The usher had made his way to the back of the auditorium and raised the house lights, triggering a roar of applause.

Andi ran her fingers through her shoulder-length hair and discreetly pressed a button on her headset to activate a hidden earpiece.

Two other grad students, Bryan Loxley and Vance McMullen, were running the show from a control room next to the test chamber. They were also watching Andi and the audience on several video screens showing closed-circuit camera views.

Vance saw Andi's signal and keyed his microphone. "Testing. Testing. One. Two. Three. Are you with us, Andi?"

She acknowledged the message by waving at a wide-eyed boy who happened to be sitting in front of a camera.

"She's done this a dozen times," Vance said. "She doesn't need our help. Do you, Andi?"

She made no reaction to the question.

"See? She doesn't need us. Let's grab a beer while she finishes," Vance said.

Andi's smile faded, and her face formed a subtle scowl until her earpiece relayed laugher from the control room.

"Vance is just kidding," Bryan said into his mic. He rarely said anything, but he must have felt the need to diffuse the situation.

Andi gritted her teeth and forced herself back into presentation mode.

"That was quite a show. Don't you agree?" She nodded.

Everyone in the audience clapped again. Most of them had a look of shock on their faces. They had just witnessed something unexplainable, even by the best scientists. It might as well have been magic.

"Does anyone have a question?"

A dozen hands shot up, but Andi pointed to a teenage boy in the middle of the auditorium.

"How much electricity does it take to open a portal?"

Andi waited for Vance to feed her the answer. "The larger the circumference of the ring, the more power it requires." She gestured toward the induction coil behind her. "Our one-meter ring requires about 1.3 megawatts to open a portal. That's enough electricity to power 200 homes for an hour." She turned to the other side of the audience and pointed to a teenage girl who had her hand raised.

"Why does it only stay open for 142 seconds?"

"Great question," she said and stalled to give Vance time to tell her the answer. "That's been the subject of research for decades, and we don't know exactly why there's such a specific limit." She paused for a second while she listened to her earpiece. "A widely supported hypothesis claims that energy is stacked in overlapping quantum states until it reaches a saturation point. When the coil can no longer absorb electricity, a portal forms and remains open until the energy dissipates."

"Would a bigger ring stay open longer?"

"Another great question." Andi stalled again. "It looks like we may have another physicist here," she teased. Laughter ran through the auditorium as Vance fed her an answer to regurgitate.

"There's a balance between the circumference of the induction coil, the ring, and the amount of energy it can store. It's all proportional, so the amount of energy stored in the quantum matrix is always just enough to keep the portal open for 142 seconds." She paused until a waving hand grabbed her attention. "What's your question?"

"What was on the end of the pole that got stuck in the hole?"

"For each weekly portal opening, we insert a payload into the Void. It's a container divided into twenty sections, each of which can be loaded with an experiment. A grant funds all Void research here at Belfore University, and it allows other universities and research institutes to conduct experiments in the Void without having to operate and maintain an induction coil of their own. They just have to provide an experiment that fits into one of the payload's compartments. Most experiments are from the graduate students and post-doctoral researchers here at the university, but about ten percent of the experiments are from other universities or corporate supporters of the grant." She paused for a second as Vance described the experiment he just ran. "One of our Ph.D. candidates is testing an electromagnetic propulsion system that, in theory, will move objects around in the Void without being attached to the end of a rigid pole, like the one we used today. Electronics don't work in the Void, so it requires a whole new set of technologies to do the most basic of tasks."

"Why won't electronics work in the Void?"

"Another good question," she said. "It's believed to be some property inherent to the Void that impedes the flow of electrons. There's also a great deal of high energy radiation similar to x-rays and gamma rays that damage electronic circuits."

"Has anyone ever been in the Void?"

"And lived to tell? No. That same radiation also destroys organic material. Until someone develops a method of shielding a person against the radiation, it would be a one-way trip."

"Andi," Vance said in her ear, laughing. "Ask him if he wants to go inside."

She made no acknowledgment.

Vance persisted. "Tell him it'll be like nothing he's ever done before."

Andi continued to ignore him.

"Tell him it'll rip his flesh off while his blood boils and every cell in his body gets its DNA shredded." Vance laughed.

"Does anyone else have a question?" Andi said to the audience. She answered a dozen more. They always asked the same questions, but Andi didn't care enough to remember the answers. That's what Bryan and Vance were for.

"We've got time for one more," she said and looked around the auditorium. An older man raised his hand. His face hardened after she pointed at him, and she knew what was about to happen. She wanted to cringe but kept an inquisitive expression.

"After decades of research and billions of dollars, why hasn't there been anything, how should I say, useful, come from this... experiment?" the man said with a German accent. "Other than a very expensive light show." He smirked.

A crooked frown formed on Andi's face. She had to deal with negative questions periodically, but this man was making a statement and throwing shade on her performance. She couldn't have that, even if she did completely agree with him. She listened for Vance to enumerate all the wonderful accomplishments Voidology had bestowed on mankind, but he didn't. All she heard was him whining in her earpiece about how offended he was by the questions, and how he was going to give that man a piece of his mind. Bryan was silent as usual.

They were both useless to her, and the countdown to embarrassment had commenced. Her lips tightened. She wanted to go back to the control room and wring their necks, but she wouldn't break character. She was just going to wing it and hope for the best.

"Three decades ago, a new scientific field was created—by accident, I might add. Voidology is so different from anything else, there wasn't a place to put it. So, this baby science was stuck under the physics umbrella even though very little in classical physics applies to the Void." She walked to the edge of the stage, directly in front of the German.

"Contrary to your statement, there have been many advances resulting from our research. The induction coils are

1,800 percent more efficient than the one used by Rutledge's original experiment. We've inspired the material sciences to create better superconductors, which have been used in countless applications. Sensor and shielding technologies have drastically improved as we try to pry the secrets out of the Void. The leader of the first Mars research team said that without the Void and the technologies it brought about, humans wouldn't be living on the red planet."

She paused to build some drama. "The first portal killed two people, but we can now routinely open portals, and they're safe enough for guests to observe without a pressure suit or risking radiation exposure."

She walked back behind the lectern, raised herself up on her toes, and rested her hands on the faux-wood surface. "I'm proud to be part of this research team. We may have to crawl before we can walk, but we're doing it." She thought she was pulling off a pretty convincing lie. "How long did it take for us to develop the Marconi into an iPhone? Over 100 years? And what about the Moon shot? We got much more from that endeavor than an extended joyride around a big, gray rock. We're on track to make the world-changing discoveries you were promised. Are you ready?" She quickly bowed her head to conclude her performance and prevent the German from asking any more questions.

There was another round of applause.

"I hope everyone enjoyed the exhibition. Please come back and see us again," Andi said.

The house curtains lowered in front of the test chamber, and the usher opened the back doors. Andi smiled and waved until the last person had left. Then she marched off straight to the control room.

CHAPTER 4

THE ASS CHEWING

Bryan and Vance were performing the final shut-down routines for the induction coil when Andi burst into the control room. Her face was red, and she pressed her lips together so tightly that her mouth looked like a penciled-line on her face.

"Can you believe that idiot?" Vance asked, oblivious to Andi's fury. He crossed his arms and leaned back in his chair. "I bet he's a geologist or some other simple-science."

Andi snarled. "I don't give a crap what he is. Your job is to answer the audience's questions, and you failed." She was almost yelling. "It's no wonder this program is such a complete joke. That German was right to question this charade. I wanted to bring him up on stage and get him a standing ovation."

Vance furrowed his eyebrows. "Dude, I'm the senior research assistant, and some glorified tour guide isn't going to barge into my lab and talk down to me." He looked over at Bryan for support, but he didn't get any.

"First of all, I'm not a dude." Andi rolled her eyes. "And second, you're not a senior anything." She crossed her arms to mock him. "This is *not* your lab, and I'm *not* a tour guide."

Vance stiffened his posture. "My research is the most important thing going on in this program. You're working for me whether you know it or not, tour guide."

"I hate to burst your little bubble, but you just ran your super important experiment for three seventh grade classes, a hungover alumni party, and a couple of Germans who think you're more of a disgrace than I do—and that's a lot."

Vance sprang out of his chair. "You... you just don't understand." He shook his head and started to walk away.

"Oh, I understand quite well." She smirked. "This program hasn't produced anything useful in its thirty-year existence besides an overpriced disco ball. Maybe you should drop out, hang that metal donut from the ceiling, and open a retro-night club." She wobbled her head to cap off her excellent burn.

Vance turned as red as his long frizzy hair and scraggly beard. "I *am* doing something important and a lot more than you are."

"Important? Are you kidding me? Are you going to add a new color to the light show?" Andi wasn't going to let a loser like Vance bully her.

Vance pointed his finger at her. "We all don't get a free ride because our daddy's the dean. You should go do something more suited to your talents and let someone more deserving take your slot."

Nothing infuriated Andi more than someone pointing their finger at her. "Are you crazy? This is the last place I want to be."

"Then why are you here?" Vance snapped.

Andi put her hands on her hips. "Because I'm going to be a famous actor."

Vance's head flinched back slightly.

"The only way I can get my father to pay for Juilliard is to fill in here until some other dupe joins the Voidology program. Or, God forbid, I end up with a Ph.D. in worthlessness. My dad is using me, and I'm using him. I'm just a fraud, and that perfectly qualifies me to be here. Don't you think?"

"You're right about being a fraud. You can't even answer questions from a bunch of kids without help," he said. "I bet the dean faked your scores to get you admitted."

"I scored higher on the GRE than you," she said with no hesitation.

"I doubt it." Vance snorted. "Besides, you have no idea how I did."

"It doesn't matter. I aced it. Did you?"

A crooked smile formed on Vance's face. "I don't believe you. You can't even be a tour guide without help."

"Believe whatever you want, but I'm just as qualified to be here as you."

An alarm sounded, and several red lights flashed on the console. Vance ran over to his keyboard and entered a sequence to finish powering down the induction coil.

"Maybe more qualified," Andi said with a snort.

"Shut up," Vance said, still typing at the console.

Andi realigned her fiery gaze on Bryan, who hadn't made a peep. "You don't have anything to say?"

There was an awkward moment of silence until he broke it. "You answered the German's question as well as we could." He never looked directly at her.

Andi stomped over to a cork bulletin board hanging on the wall. She wished she had worn less comfortable shoes, so the sound of her feet would punctuate her mood. She ripped off a pamphlet, causing a pushpin to skip across the control room's floor.

"I recited this ridiculous propaganda," she said, holding up a glossy, tri-fold brochure the university used to boost exhibition attendance. She then flung it at them. It didn't travel far, but it spun around in the air like a wounded bird struggling to fly.

A buzz came from Andi's pocket, interrupting the performance. She whipped out her phone and read the new message. Her confident expression faded.

"Thanks so much for all of your wonderful help," she said as sarcastically as she could.

She slammed the door on her way out.

CHAPTER 5

THE CRISIS OF FAITH

A thin figure glided through a lengthy corridor connecting the main complex of the Church to its sanctuary. Her white robe reached the floor. Its hood obscured her face, and her hands were tucked deep inside its pockets. The low light created the appearance of an apparition haunting the passageway, but Nancy was flesh and blood, and she was on the final leg of her journey.

Nancy was part of the Church's top echelon. She was an acolyte, one of twelve, and headed an adjunct conclave dedicated to deciphering the mysteries of the Void. Her faith in the Church was unshakable, and her skills were unmatched by anyone in the congregation except for the Prophet. She wore a golden circle, the symbol of the Church, on her lapel. The Prophet had only bestowed a handful of such honors to recognize great contributions to the Church, and she wore it proudly. But despite her best efforts, the research she managed had reached an impasse.

Modeling the Void with a new form of mathematics had been Nancy's idea. It was challenging, but the approach seemed promising. Everyone believed she could do it, even the Prophet. She became so wrapped up in the idea of being the one who delivered the solution, she missed how far off target her work had become. Her string of successes turned into a contradicting mangle of equations she would never resolve. The hopelessness of her work felt like a weight pushing her into the ground. The Church once gave her comfort, but now, it was crushing her.

The Prophet had saved Nancy from a miserable existence. He found her and provided her a new life in the Church, one where she excelled. She wanted so badly to repay him. This desire burned in her and pushed her to be the best acolyte in the Church, but her faith and perseverance weren't enough. She couldn't complete her task. She didn't think anyone could. The Prophet might understand her failure and give her a second chance, but she had never known him to forgive.

She slowed her pace after entering the sanctuary. It was a fifty-foot-tall geodesic dome formed out of thousands of interlocking glass panes. Sunlight streamed in and cast a long shadow off of a platform, a dais, in its center. Steps led to the top of the structure where a gilded throne seated a middle-aged man wearing an elaborate white robe.

"Do you want to see the face of God, child?" The Prophet asked, staring down at Nancy.

She had bowed her head as soon as she entered the sanctuary and didn't look up to answer. "We all do, Prophet. It is our life."

"Then why have you interrupted my meditation?" His tone was full of scorn.

"The simulation is complete, Prophet." She spoke quickly. "The results are ready for you to review."

"Show me," he demanded.

Nancy pulled a small tablet out of her robe's pocket. She hesitated but climbed a few steps and reached up to hand him the device. He snatched it from her, and she retreated to the bottom. She kept her eyes lowered, but she heard the Prophet tapping on the screen to flip through the pages of formulas and graphs.

His hand stilled, and then the tablet struck the black marble floor beside her. She took a quick step back, crunching glass under her foot before she regained control of herself.

The Prophet stood and descended the steps. "Your work is contributing nothing to the Church. I declare your conclave dissolved." He paused for a second. "I will no longer give you the opportunity to fail me."

Nancy couldn't face his gaze.

The Prophet pulled back her hood and lifted her head, forcing her to look him in the eyes. He smiled, and she thought for a second that he might show some compassion, but he struck her with the back of his hand instead. She stumbled to her knees and clasped her face. Her mind flashed back to her life before the Church. The violence and subjugation were now the same.

"When was your last communion, child?"

"Six months, Prophet." Her voice quivered.

"God will not accept failure, and neither will I." He snapped his fingers, and two barrel-chested men dressed in white uniforms appeared and yanked her off the floor. She had landed on the fragments of glass, and her once pristine robe had growing spots of blood.

"Don't bother with the sacramental cassock," the Prophet said as he climbed the steps to his throne.

Nancy sobbed as the guards dragged her away. She no longer clung to the hope of redeeming herself. The Prophet had issued her a death sentence.

"Don't cry, child," he said. "You will meet God sooner than you expected."

CHAPTER 6

THE PROBATION

"Hi, Andi," the dean's receptionist said. "I haven't seen you in a month."

"Hey, Mary, I've been busy."

"I bet. How's the presenter gig going? Didn't you just finish an exhibition?"

Andi laughed. "I'm amazed they got by before I took it over. Vance and Bryan are definitely not presentation material."

"I heard you do a great job. We've even had an uptick in attendance."

"Thanks." Andi smiled. "But we only had seventy-eight today."

"It's been years since I've seen the Void show. I'll make sure to come next week."

Andi lowered her voice. "You don't by chance know why I've been summoned?"

The receptionist shook her head, but Andi didn't believe she would tell her, anyway.

The door behind the Mary clicked and opened, and Dean Richard Fyffe stepped out. "I was about to send you another message."

"Hey, Dad." Andi cocked her head and waited for a proper greeting.

Instead, the dean just motioned her into his office.

"I just finished your dog and pony show," she said. "You're lucky I hadn't left campus."

Professor Thomas Rutledge sat in one of the two chairs in front of the dean's desk. Andi used all of her self-control to keep from rolling her eyes at him. He only worked for Belfore because his dead father discovered the Void, forever ago. The prodigal son was smart enough to parlay his lineage into becoming a department head, but other than that, he was an egocentric bureaucrat in charge of a failed program. Her knowledge of the Void was greater than his, and that wasn't saying much.

"Miss Fyffe," Rutledge said, but he remained in his seat.

The dean shut the door and slid his glasses down to the tip of his nose. "Tom has brought to my attention that we have a problem."

"What?" Andi asked with an artificial look of surprise.

The dean frowned. "Don't be flippant, Andalusia."

Of course, she knew what he talking about, but she shook her head. She wanted to give that snitch Rutledge a piece of her mind, but that would have to wait.

Rutledge looked at Andi with disdain. "You're failing Dimensional Physics and High Energy Magnetics."

Andi made a dismissive wave. "They're complete bores."

"That's two-thirds of your course load," Rutledge said.

"I'll make it up. I've just been spending a lot of time at rehearsals and haven't had time to learn the material."

Rutledge almost laughed but tamped it down to a snort. "You're failing because of a play?"

Andi stared at him but didn't respond. She didn't care what his opinion of her was.

"It's my job as department head to make sure the university meets all grant requirements, and I can't do that without the minimum number of students in the program," Rutledge said. "If you fail, so goes our grant."

"If you're so concerned about your precious grant, why don't you get your department to do something novel, like make a discovery or solve a problem. You guys are a complete joke." Andi felt her nostrils flaring and was about to continue her dress down, but her dad interrupted.

"Sweetheart, our deal was that I'll pay for Juilliard if, and only if, you help keep the grant active. Failing just one class disqualifies you." He crossed his arms. "And you're failing two."

"I'll try harder, but this physics stuff is not really my thing. Shouldn't someone be inflating my grades, you know, for the greater good? You're the dean after all."

Her father let out a sigh. "Dishonesty is against our code. Besides, you have a bachelor's degree in physics. You're capable of doing the work."

"My degree is in classical physics because you made me get it. At least it has practical applications, unlike Voidology." She glanced at Rutledge to see if her dig had any teeth. "And if you recall, I also have two other degrees."

Rutledge laughed out loud this time. "A fine arts degree and a language degree will not help you here." He looked over at the dean. "I told you it was a bad idea to bring her into the program."

"If you recall, Tom, you weren't able to find anybody, and I had to step in and resolve the problem," the dean said and rubbed his brow.

Andi was surprised by her father's effort to defend her. "I'll make more of an effort as soon as my play ends."

"You're an understudy," the dean said. "They'll be fine without you."

"What?" She couldn't believe her own father insulted her like that. What happened to him defending her?

"You can't spend all of your time at the theater if it's causing you to fail. There's a lot at stake here, and we've already been through this."

"But, Dad, I can't bail on my theater group. I made a commitment."

"What are the chances the performance will need an understudy?"

Andi flared out her fingers. "I'm everyone's understudy, so it's definitely a possibility."

"It doesn't matter. You have a prior commitment to this program." He pushed his glasses up to their normal position. "And you will honor it."

Andi bounced what her father had said around in her head. She decided it was better to agree with him and carry on as she had been rather than continue the argument. She hadn't been studying, that was true. Maybe a little more effort on her part was necessary, and she needed his money for Juilliard. "Okay, I'll get everything back on track. Don't worry."

"I'm sure you will. Until then, I'm assigning a tutor to help you improve your grades."

Andi shook her head. "That's not going to work for me."

"I don't think you understand how important this grant is to Belfore. I believe it's the best course of action at this point."

Andi started to speak, but the dean held up his hand to stop her. "Having a tutor may be exactly what you need, and you might learn something."

Andi took a deep breath. "Okay, but I'm not expecting this to be beneficial for anyone." Especially for the tutor, if she had anything to say about it.

"You'll need to change your attitude to make this work," the dean said.

While she pretended to mull over what he said, she stared at a picture on his desk. It was from when she was in high school, and she was wearing a cheerleading uniform and holding two big pom-poms. Next to it was a photo of her mother dressed as Lady Macbeth in a medieval dress holding a bouquet of red roses. Andi had the same picture hanging in her apartment. She could hear her mother telling her she could do anything if she put her mind to it. The sound of her voice was so clear it was like she was in the office. The picture gave her the strength to follow her own dreams and not her father's. Her mother was still helping her, even if she had been gone for a decade.

"I'll arrange your first tutoring session," the dean said, "and I'll be monitoring your progress."

"Sounds great, Dad," she lied and left his office.

CHAPTER 7

THE REHEARSAL

Rehearsal for the Dark Crowd Players began at 7:00 p.m. Andi arrived early and nearly ran into a slim man dressed in black as she entered the theater.

"It's nice to see someone here on time," the director said. "Sadly, it's just the understudy."

Andi put on a cheery face. "Do you think there's any—"

"No, dear," he interrupted and shook his head.

Andi wasn't giving up. "I'll do any part. I know all the lines."

"I'm sure you do." He wrinkled up his nose. "Why don't you go do something useful, like cleaning the green room?" He walked away before she could respond.

Andi stared at the director's back. If he never let her act, he would never change his opinion of her. He infuriated her, but she grabbed a mop and bucket from a closet and headed to the green room. Mumbling to herself about the futility of her situation, she discovered that she wasn't the only one who had arrived on time.

"Oh, hi, Andi," said Alisha, a twenty-five-year-old starlet-wannabe, relaxing on a threadbare, velvet sofa.

"Hey, Alisha. Why aren't you out front? David thought I was the only one here."

Alisha leered. "He knows I'm here."

Andi dropped the mop bucket a little too hard, splashing water on the floor. Did the director and Alisha have something going on? Is this how she got her role? She couldn't help wondering if Juilliard was this way, but it didn't matter because she would be in New York City and not some Podunk college town like Belfore.

"Can you be a sweetie and get me a Diet Coke?" Alisha's tone was more of an order than a request.

Andi's eyebrows rose. "Isn't there one in the fridge?"

"I haven't checked." Alisha inspected the polish on her nails.

Andi leaned the mop handle against the wall and opened the mini-fridge. There was a case of the drink inside. She grabbed one and handed it to Alisha, a mere three feet away.

"This is too warm. Can you get me some ice?"

Andi let out a sigh but forced a smile on her face. "Sure. Be right back."

Andi had to be part of the production long enough to show off her acting abilities. Otherwise, she was just the maid, one who didn't get paid. If keeping the director's girlfriend happy was the price she had to pay, she had to do it. She ran across the street and bought a Diet Coke with ice from a fast-food restaurant. She returned to an empty green room, so she stuck the straw in her mouth and claimed it for herself. The awful taste of artificial sweetener summarized her mood.

It took Andi less than an hour to get the green room spotless. The players were only rehearsing the second act, and she had missed most of the performance. In the few minutes she saw, Alisha ad-libbed her lines twice and had to be prompted another time. The director hated that kind of unprofessional behavior, but now Andi understood how Alisha escaped his wrath.

After most of the actors left, Andi approached the director. "David, would it be okay if I missed a couple of rehearsals this week? I've really got to catch up on my studies."

"Andrea, if you can't commit to the players, then don't come here anymore. You must be serious if you want to succeed as an actor."

"All I do is clean up after everyone and get drinks. Surely you can make it one day without me."

"I guess this is goodbye then." David raised his chin and walked away. "Adieu."

Andi's posture wilted as she tried to figure out a way to both catch up on her classes and make rehearsals. She didn't know how to do it, but she wouldn't ditch her dream for that stupid grant. "Never mind. I'll be here."

CHAPTER 8

THE SUPER POWER

Andi's phone started beeping at five-thirty in the morning. Fumbling around to turn it off, she knocked it to the floor. It continued to beep. She let out a sleepy sigh but knew it was for the best since she would avoid an endless ten-minute snooze cycle. For once, she couldn't miss her 8:00 a.m. Dimensional Physics class, and she planned to cram in some extra study time before it started. She rolled out of bed and fished around on the floor for her phone. She silenced the alarm, but the colony of dust bunnies disgusted her.

Andi had a one-bedroom apartment just off-campus. It was part of the deal she negotiated with her father to keep the grant going. She lived above an elderly woman, Mrs. Nelms, who seemed helpless in every way except for her counterintelligence-grade spying. Andi was ninety-eight percent certain that her father used the grandma to monitor her activities. She laughed to herself about having the time to enjoy something worth reporting to her father. The joke was on them.

After a quick shower, Andi grabbed her tablet and a breakfast bar and headed out the door. She crept down the steps and was opening her car door when the kerchunk of a deadbolt broke the silence. A door opened, and a puffy Pomeranian stuck its head out, followed by a short woman wearing cat-eye glasses and a housecoat. Andi jumped into her car and closed the door when the barking dog charged her. She wanted to drive away and ignore the old bag, but she rolled her window down instead.

"You're leaving awfully early, aren't you?"

"Good morning, Mrs. Nelms. I'm going to get some early studying in."

"Oh, that's good, dear. You go on and get to school." She waved goodbye, and her dog ran back inside.

Andi drove off so quickly her tires chirped on the asphalt. She smiled because she knew that if she flunked out, the spy would lose whatever her father, or the grant, paid her. It wasn't just Mrs. Nelms, either. Vance, Bryan, the twins, and Rutledge were all dependent on Andi passing her classes. If Belfore lost the grant, most of its dependents could do something else but not Rutledge. Losing the grant would be more than his father's reputation could overcome. She smiled again at the thought of ending his career.

It would've taken Andi fifteen minutes to walk to class, but driving her Prius was more in line with the image she wanted to maintain. She had not, however, been on campus so early and was delighted to find an abundance of parking spots. Trolling for a spot usually took at least twenty minutes, and she now had bonus time. Her day was off to an auspicious beginning until she reached the language lab, and it hadn't opened.

Andi sat on the floor by the entrance and ate her breakfast bar while waiting for someone to show up and unlock the lab.

"It's about time someone got here," she said when the attendant arrived.

"The lab doesn't open until seven o'clock." He fumbled with his keys and opened the door.

"I've been waiting for almost forty-five minutes," she said. "I was about to find somewhere else to study."

The attendant smiled and flipped a light switch. Except for her early arrival, he found nothing unusual about Andi's presence.

She hadn't taken a language class in three semesters, but she was still their most regular user of the facility. Since nobody complained, and she was a dean's daughter, the attendants never turned her away. They wondered about her affinity for the lab, but she would never tell them why.

It was her secret.

Andi spent much of her undergraduate career in the language labs. She had mastered French, German, and Russian in record time, but learning foreign languages was not the reason she logged so many hours there. In her French 101 class, she discovered that she possessed a knack for languages. When she sealed herself in one of the soundproof cubicles to do her lab exercises, she could absorb information like a sponge.

This ability was like having a photographic memory, but she didn't recall images. She could playback sound bites and audio clips and quickly discovered that her talent extended beyond learning languages. As long as she remained completely focused while she listened, she could recall it with perfect fidelity.

She used her phone to record lectures and then listened to them in one of the cubicles. Doubling or tripling the playback speed didn't affect her recall. She got audiobooks for literature classes and read aloud her textbooks and notes for the others. It didn't matter what the source was as long as she heard it and could remain focused on the sound with no distractions. Her only limitation was time.

After almost an hour, Andi packed her tablet, straightened up the cubicle, and prepared to go to her class. She had absorbed a great deal of information, but she still hadn't caught up on the material. It was just a start.

Dimensional Physics, the bane of Andi's GPA, was the study of how energy and matter behaved inside the Void. In its thirty-year existence, the fledgling field had created more questions than it had answered. Even the course name was a joke. Scientists first believed portals bridged our reality to another dimension, but that theory didn't even rank in the top three anymore. Yet the name remained. Dimensional Physics also won the contest for being the most boring, uninteresting thing Andi had ever been exposed to, and she was about to endure another hour and fifteen minutes of its torture.

She pressed a finger on her temple to quell the psychosomatic headache she was experiencing. The worst part, she thought, was that this cutting-edge field of study was a hoax. There were no models for how anything worked, and almost everything about Void physics was mere speculation. A bunch of eggheads made a bunch of guesses, and collective denial kept the lie alive. She could make a guess that there was nothing in the Void and would be just as correct as the rest.

Andi was the first arrival for the eight o'clock class, something that had never happened before. Even though she was the only one from the grant program, there were a dozen other students taking the course. They were all working on graduate degrees in more conventional studies such as classical physics or engineering. Andi thought they were trying to fluff up their transcripts or learn some über-nerd topic to impress their friends. She despised them all, even their friends.

The professor always ran five minutes behind, and Andi usually exploited four of those minutes if she showed up at all. She always found a seat in the back row to hide her disinterest, but this time she sat front and center. She was ready to absorb. After six minutes of waiting for someone else to show up, she began to wonder where everyone was. Then she noticed a message written on the whiteboard: "DP 523 - Canceled." She let out a shriek and left the classroom. Embarrassing as it was, she did have a feeling of joy over not having to endure the lecture. When her phone buzzed, she feared that someone had witnessed her mistake and was about to poke fun at her.

But it was something much worse.

CHAPTER 9

THE SUITED MAN

An overweight man marched into the sanctuary. He wore a dark gray suit with a blue tie and matching pocket square. The jacket buttons strained, but he kept the appearance of a respectable businessman. His attire was out of place among the white robes at the Church, but he wasn't like the others. Publicly, he was the face of the Church's business affairs, but his real job was to manage the Prophet.

"Why is Nancy preparing for her final communion?" he asked.

"I don't have to explain myself to you," the Prophet said, looking down at him from his perch atop the dais.

"She's your best topology expert. If you want to uncover the secrets of the Void, don't kill your best talent."

The Prophet clenched the arms of his throne. "Continued failure wears heavily on the congregation, and I can't allow that. This acolyte can inspire and motivate the others with a demonstration of complete faith."

"You spew that crap so much that I think you believe it. She's your chief physicist who's gotten you closer than anyone else here to solving the equations. We need her. You need her." He paused for his advice to sink in. "Our plan was to make a breakthrough before anyone else and cash in. Isn't that what you still want?"

The Prophet gazed out the faceted windows of the geodesic dome. "We must take steps to prevent the acolyte's loss of faith from metastasizing in the other conclaves."

"I'll remind you again that everyone has failed to solve those stupid equations, including you. She's the best you've got, and she's the best you can get."

"I can't allow the best acolyte to fail, or we'll lose the rest. A final communion will elevate her in the eyes of my followers, and her sacrifice will strengthen the Church. Call it redemption if it makes you feel better."

The suited man shook his head. "You're throwing away your best person. Wasting her talents, and for what? To play your stupid cult game?"

"She is not my best person. She's my best failure." He smiled. "Do your job and find a replacement."

Even after years of wrangling the so-called spiritual leader, the suited man strained to keep his composure.

"From what I understand," the Prophet said, "there are two other expert researchers at Belfore. Twins, I believe. I've studied their research, and their grasp of the Void is much greater than that of our failed acolyte."

The suited man nodded. "Yes. The brother and sister team are as far along as we are regarding the modeling equations. Belfore could jump ahead of us."

"That's remarkable for a third-rate institution," the Prophet scoffed. "The moths are still drawn to the flame I ignited.

The suited man tried to hold back a snort but ended up clearing his throat to cover up his reaction.

"Why haven't you acquired these twins for me?"

"Our intel suggests that they're not viable candidates for the Church, brilliant but incompatible with our methods."

"We can already access their research," the Prophet said. "Don't buy the cow when the milk is free."

"It's unfortunate that they can't utilize our databases. It might speed this process along." The suited man looked at his tablet. "There is one other research track at Belfore on intra-Void propulsion. Is that something you wish to take possession of?"

"It's completely worthless," the Prophet said without hesitation. "There will never be a need to move around in the Void."

"Are you sure? The researcher is having financial problems, so he's an ideal candidate for the Church."

The Prophet shook his head. "Who else?" he demanded.

"The only other choice at Belfore is their newest student." The suited man pressed his lips together. "But she's flunking most of her classes. If she's kicked out of the program, the number of required students falls below the minimum requirement and will invalidate the grant."

"Perhaps we're devoting too many of our resources to extinguishing Belfore's miserable existence. They seem to fail all on their own."

The suited man nodded, finally agreeing with something the Prophet said.

"I find it amusing that such a *prestigious* university has only two research tracks. What sort of world-leading Voidology program is this? We run over a hundred, and that's not counting the parallel variants," the Prophet boasted.

"It's possible that your grand plan has worked too well."

"I'll not lose any sleep over Belfore's demise."

"But without the grant, we'll lose access to the twins' research and also the Church's primary source of income."

"That's precisely why we need to motivate the congregation and complete our work."

"Getting rid of Nancy will not help us win this race."

"I have complete confidence that we'll prevail. If Belfore appears to be on the verge of a breakthrough, I'll simply pull the plug on them before it's published."

"And how will you do that?" The suited man was almost afraid to ask.

"You need to pay more attention to the Void-tech we've amassed over the years. The perfect weapon to quite literally remove Belfore from the map is in our arsenal, and I won't hesitate to use it." Just speaking about Belfore's annihilation made the Prophet smile.

The suited man's concern was justified, but it was his job to prevent the Prophet from getting out of control. "Don't forget that the grant's requirement for Belfore to use renewable energy has made our solar farm lucrative. We can't afford to lose our only client."

"Green energy usage is on the rise. We'll always be able to find other clients to sell our premium, guilt-free product to. Besides, we'll be the most popular tech company in the world when the Void can be properly exploited."

"I hope you're right."

"Schedule the communion ceremony," the Prophet said. "We need to promote the acolyte as soon as possible."

"Her name is Nancy." The suited man frowned. He had no objections to killing the acolyte. He just wanted to impress upon the Prophet how difficult it would be to find a replacement in a world with dwindling interest in the Void. But, as long as the Church continued to make him a wealthy man, he would do whatever the Prophet required of him.

CHAPTER 10

THE FIRE

Andi bit her lip as she read the message on her phone a second time. It was bad enough that she arrived early to a canceled class, but the message made it worse. Her father had arranged her first tutoring session, and it began in ten minutes in the induction coil's control room. She didn't know about the canceled class, and he did. That irritated her. She took in a deep breath and slowly exhaled. The message continued to say that she would meet twice a day with the tutor until the grant was out of jeopardy. She squeezed her eyelids shut as she tried to calculate how this new burden would impact her schedule. She didn't like it.

Andi made her way across campus to the control room, the same room where she lectured Bryan and Vance for hanging her out to dry during the last exhibition. When she reached her destination, she paused outside the doorway to psych herself up. She could only guess who would be waiting.

Her father might have recruited a faculty member or someone else in the program, but his options were limited. With her current run of luck, she needed to prepare for the worst, also known as Vance.

Andi stiffened her expression and flung the door open. Her insides melted, but she maintained strength in her exterior. Vance swiveled his chair around and smirked.

She screamed on the inside, but he wasn't going to see her anguish. She cocked her head to one side and said, "Great. It's you." She drew the last word out and imbued it with as much loathing as she could squeeze into it.

Vance burst into laughter. "Dude, get real. They wouldn't put the top dog on dunce duty."

"Aren't those wonder twins the top dogs around here? At the exhibitions, they're who everybody asks about. Nobody's ever wanted to know about you." She didn't know much about the twins, but she was telling the truth about the audience's interest and knew it would pinch Vance's enlarged ego.

"I've had more success lately than they have." Vance's posture was rigid now, and he clenched his teeth. "You would know that if you ever paid attention to *anything*."

"Oh no, it looks like I struck a nerve," she said in a whiny little voice.

"You don't know anything, dunce." He swiveled his chair around to face his computer screen.

Andi laughed. "I know this loser program can't get five students on its own merit. How crazy unpopular would something have to be for that? Isn't this supposed to be the best program of its kind in the world?"

"Not everyone's cut out for such advanced research. It's just too difficult for most people, like you." He didn't turn around to look at Andi, but his volume increased.

"Do you think someone is going to hire you with your precious degree in Worthless-ology?" She was having too much fun to back down.

"Just because you can't understand the value of this program doesn't mean others don't." He shook his head.

"But you see," Andi said in her most scornful tone, "I do understand. You're a small cog in a giant con job that's desperately sucking on the government's teat. You pretend to do your research under the guise of one day discovering something useful while you drain the grant dry."

Vance still didn't turn around, but his voice lowered. "We have made discoveries."

"Um-hum. I've read the marketing brochure."

Vance let out an exasperated sigh. "You don't deserve to be here."

"I don't want to be here, either. But it's not beneath me to use your grant to get what I want. That's how this department works. Isn't it?" She slapped her hands together loud enough to make him jump. "You better start paying me a little more respect because I could blow this whole tutoring thing off, fail, and end the grant. Then you would have nothing." She smiled to herself but couldn't stop her harangue. "That makes me the top dog around here."

Vance shoved his chair away from the computer and swung around to face her. "You're not getting my respect," he said, approaching a shout. "You're failing your classes, and you've already killed the program. Nobody ever thought you would help save the grant."

Andi felt a vein pulsing in her head. She wanted to run across the room and slap Vance's smug face, but something stopped her. Vance had unknowingly sparked an ember inside her and fanned it into a flame. She wasn't going to let him be right. How dare he presume anything about her? She would make him and everyone else eat their words. It didn't matter how much effort it would take.

She was about to launch another salvo at Vance when Bryan walked in behind her.

"Hi, Andi. Are you ready for some tutoring?" His eyes darted to the floor while he waited for her reply.

Andi forced a smile. "Sure. Let's get started."

CHAPTER 11

THE TUTORING SESSION

Andi followed Bryan to a conference room on the second floor. She had never noticed how short he was and thought he looked like a child from behind. He always wore a white button-up shirt and black pants. It was more professional looking than the worn-out T-shirt and jeans Vance wore every day, but it was odd for a college student. His bowl-cut hair was the worst, though. It was jet black and in need of some conditioner. She could really help him with his appearance, probably more than he could help her with Voidology.

"I scheduled the room for two hours." His voice was quiet and unimposing, the very opposite of Vance. "We'll need to find a different place next time." He sat at the conference table, and Andi took a seat across from him.

"Were you forced to do this?" Andi wanted to explore the parameters of the arrangement and see what she had to work with.

"As a research assistant, I'm an employee of the department." He stared down at the table.

"You're going to have to look at me when you're talking. I can barely understand what you're saying."

He glanced up at her. "Okay." But he looked back down at the table.

"Up here." She pointed at her eyes, wondering if he was shy or intimidated.

He followed her command.

"Is this tutoring thing something you wanted to do?" she asked, trying to keep his focus.

"I don't mind helping if the program's at stake." He looked her in the eyes for a moment but returned to staring at the table.

"Don't you have an experiment or something to prepare for?"

He looked back up at her. "Vance and the twins get most of the time with the coil. They have seniority."

"Those experiments will fail," she scoffed.

"They don't all fail. Vance's propulsion system is the most impressive physical experiment I've seen with the Void. He's only a few tries away from having something remarkable."

Andi raised her eyebrows. "Really?" She didn't know if she should be upset that Vance was actually accomplishing something or happy about having more to hold over him.

"Yes." Bryan continued to look her in the eyes. "Vance is the best at what he does. Also, the twins are creating a mathematical model of the Void's topology. They could be the next Einstein or Hawking."

She leaned forward in her chair. "What is it with those *twins?* Do they even exist?"

Bryan smiled. "Yes, of course, they do. They share an office on the seventh floor."

"I've never seen them at an exhibition or anywhere else as far as that goes. I was beginning to think my father had manufactured a couple of fictitious students just to keep the grant going."

"They're real, and nobody's as close as they are to solving the topology equations."

"Hmm." Andi would have to adjust some of her preconceptions. "How come I've never met them?"

"They're reclusive—and they don't relate well to other people."

"If you say so." Andi struggled not to grin.

Bryan nodded. "They're only into their mathematics, and people aren't very mathematical."

Andi frowned. "I was really hoping they weren't real, and they could make up some fake person to take my place."

"I can introduce you to them if you want."

"Sure," she said. "They'd probably like to meet me too."

"Maybe." He looked down at the table for a second.

"So, if everything is so great in the Voidology department, why is the grant in jeopardy?"

"After thirty years, Void research isn't the shiny new thing. Everyone wants to go to Mars or make quantum computers."

"Why would such a gigantic grant only require five students in the university's program?"

"The grant has minimum requirements because they wanted to encourage universities of all sizes to have research programs. Belfore got the bulk of the grant because this is where the discovery was made, but their program requirements are the same as everyone else's. We just have to run a weekly portal opening and support research from other universities."

"Belfore has become too dependent on the grant. Everything here revolves around it."

"The grant is extraordinary. Nothing like it had ever been done before. Governments, commercial entities, and academia all wanted to invest heavily in Void research to accelerate its development."

Andi tried not to laugh. "Well, that's been a giant fail."

"Science sometimes takes time, and there are still people interested in the research."

"In my six weeks of running the exhibition, I've seen three types of people. The field trip students who are forced to come, the visiting alumni who got on the wrong tour, and the doubting scientists who wanted to confirm their suspicions. If you want the program to be taken seriously, you need to find something useful to do with that big metal donut other than put on an overpriced light show."

Bryan started to speak but hesitated.

"Go on, there's no reason to be shy around me," Andi said, trying to coax out his response.

"You may not want it," Bryan said and looked down at the table again, "but I'll give you some advice."

"Let me have it." She made a beckoning gesture with her hand.

Bryan hesitated again but then continued. "That *donut* represents decades of research, and it's funding a significant portion of this entire university. If you want to get along with everyone here, don't call it a donut."

Andi pondered what he said for a second and groaned. If she was going to show everyone who was really steering this ship, she needed to play nice until she was on a better footing. "Okay. I'll stop calling it a donut. Anything else?"

Bryan hesitated for a second. "You could give Vance a break."

Andi laughed. "Why would I do that?"

"He works a lot harder than you think, and he's accomplished more than anyone except for the twins. He also works two other jobs to pay his tuition."

"No guarantees on that one," she said.

After an awkward pause, Bryan changed the subject back to tutoring. "Dimensional Physics isn't that hard. If you did as well as you say you did on the entrance exams, it shouldn't be a problem for you."

"I never said it was hard." She shook her head. "I said it was boring, and I didn't have time to learn the material."

Bryan's eyes widened. "I think it's the most fascinating subject there is. I've dedicated my life to it. Don't you want to know what's in the Void?"

Andi shook her head. "It seems as if you've drunk the Kool-Aid. All you believers will support further research no matter how much failure there is."

"You talk like Voidology is a cult."

"Well?" She looked at him with her eyebrows raised.

"It's science. You theorize, create hypotheses, experiment, and prove or disprove your assumptions."

"It's a black hole in the middle of a big metal... ring."

"It's beautiful," he said.

Andi decided she would give up while she was ahead and brought up the Dimensional Physics textbook on her tablet.

"You never answered my question," Bryan said.

Andi looked him in the eyes.

"Which question?"

"Don't you want to know what's in the Void?"

She laughed. "I already know what's in there. Nothing." She held up her hand and made a zero with her thumb and fingers.

"You don't think it goes to another place?"

"Well if it does, nothing survives in there, so it won't be a nice place."

"We'll have shielding one day to protect us."

"You sound awfully confident."

"Have some faith." Bryan looked directly at her and smiled.

* * *

Andi looked at her watch for the first time since her tutoring session began and couldn't believe two hours had passed. She thought compulsory tutoring would be a complete waste of her time, and she had even devised an exit strategy. She had planned to wait ten minutes and convince her tutor, mostly by browbeating, that it would be best to end the session early. But she didn't need to escape.

Bryan was quite knowledgeable of Dimensional Physics and could explain the basics of the subject with far greater clarity than Andi's textbooks or professors. She saw his passion for the subject, and he was somehow the secret sauce for making her understand it. He helped her piece the sound clips floating in her mind together in such a way that they transformed into something useful.

"I think I understand this boring dribble better now."

Bryan almost looked back down at the table but stopped. "You're welcome," he said, though it sounded more like a question than a statement.

"Yeah, yeah. Thanks for your help." She smiled.

"Honestly, Andi, I didn't expect you to pick up the material as quickly as you did."

"Oh, that's just because I studied this morning. It was the first time I've spent quality time trying to learn it, but it didn't make much sense until you went through it with me."

"Really?"

Andi nodded.

"It took me a whole semester to learn the mapping equations, and you could recite them from memory."

She shrugged. "What can I say?" She had no intention of telling him about her secret ability, but she might have tipped her hand by showing too much improvement.

"According to my instructions, we need to have another session later today on High Energy Magnetics." He looked down at the table.

"Hmm." Andi mashed her lips together until they turned into a frown. "I'll be really busy tonight. I have to be at rehearsal, or the director will replace me."

Bryan still looked down at the table. "I'll get into serious trouble if we don't have another session."

Andi's face brightened with an idea. "Do you know where the Dark Crowd Players Theater is?"

Bryan looked back up at her and shook his head.

"Let's meet there tonight during my rehearsal." She smiled at having fed two birds with one scone.

"How can we have a tutoring session if you're rehearsing?"

"I'm just the understudy, but everyone seems to always make it there." She let out a sigh. "I just pick up after the actors and clean the theater while they rehearse, but I have to be there." She paused. "Acting is important to me."

"What's the play?"

"*The Tempest.*" She smiled.

"Shakespeare." Bryan groaned. "I imagine it will put me to sleep."

"Good grief," she said. "You need to learn how to appreciate the arts."

"I appreciate the Void," he said with all seriousness.

Andi mocked his groan.

"Whose part do you fill in for?"

"All of them." She smiled.

"You know the whole play?"

"Well, yes," she said matter-of-factly.

"Every part? That's incredible."

"How else could I be the understudy for all the parts?"

He looked back up at her. "Do you have a photographic memory?"

She paused for a second and shook her head. "No."

"That was an uncharacteristically short response."

"I don't know what you're talking about," she said.

"What I would give to have an eidetic memory." His eyes were wide. "It would make my life so much easier. I could run several projects at the same time. I would be smart enough to solve the mysteries of the Void. I would change the world."

"That's an uncharacteristically long response," she parodied. "Besides, if I had a photographic memory, why is my own father about to kick me out of the program for failing a couple of classes?"

"Well—" Bryan started.

"I was being rhetorical," Andi interrupted. "Sheesh. I assure you I can't take pictures with my mind and recall the images at will." She technically told him the truth.

"If you say so," Bryan capitulated.

"The theater's in my favorite part of downtown on Maple and First Avenue."

"Is it across the street from a burger place?"

"Then you know where it is?"

Bryan laughed. "Yes, but only because Vance flips burgers there."

"I've been in that dive a dozen times," she said. "I've never seen him."

"I know." He couldn't help looking back down at the table.

"What? Has he seen me?"

Bryan nodded.

She snorted. "Well, I won't be going back there again."

CHAPTER 12

THE SACRIFICE

The Prophet indoctrinated his followers into believing the Void was a necessary step in their path to salvation. He used the transcendental experience to lure new members and reward significant contributions. It was no accident that the protective suits were the Prophet's first gift to the Church. He developed them to make a baptism in the Void possible and cement his hold over the congregation. But communion wasn't always positive reinforcement, as Nancy was about to experience.

The only part of the Church's facility large enough to hold the entire congregation was the communion hall. A sea of black marble tiled the floor, and a white wall encircled the cavernous space. Its domed ceiling was featureless except for large golden circles marking the cardinal directions. The Prophet was the centerpiece, surrounded by his followers. He stood atop a fifteen-foot-tall transparent chamber showcasing a gray metal ring. It was an induction coil, over a meter in diameter and held tangentially between two bollards rising out of the floor. The entire structure slowly rotated, giving the appearance of a giant eye sweeping its gaze across the crowd.

"God has called upon one of our most cherished acolytes," the Prophet boomed. "She will make the leap you fear and give your faith a path to follow."

The platform rotated, but he turned around three hundred and sixty degrees to peer down on the entire flock.

"More than any other, she has poured her soul into the Church."

No one below would doubt the proclamation.

"I do not wish to let her go, but she has the canonical right to answer God's calling. I cannot deny her that privilege." He paused and clasped his hands over his heart.

The crowd hung on his every word.

"Our acolyte's conviction has earned her final communion. Something you should all aspire."

Like an angler, he set the hook.

"You cannot lose your soul for eternity. You must strive to reach her level of faith." His voice grew louder. "You must take her place and learn the secrets of the Void. You can only find God by committing your life to our cause."

A triggered chant came from his congregation. "It is our life."

The Prophet closed his eyes and lowered the volume of his voice. "She will be deeply missed." A crocodile tear rolled down his cheek. He wiped his face and pressed his palms together. The crowd followed his lead, and everyone bowed their heads for a silent prayer until the hall's floor began to vibrate.

As the induction coil finished its charging cycle, swirling neon lights became visible inside the chamber and intensified. The colorful lights of the Rutledge effect bathed the followers until the ring released a bright flash and opened a portal to the Void.

The Prophet stretched his hands up, fingers splayed. "Acolyte," he shouted with zeal, "God awaits you."

Thirty feet above the platform, a hatch in the dome irised open and a cylindrical-shaped object, the immersion capsule, lowered into the communion hall. It hung from the end of a rigid pole stretching back up through the aperture. The capsule was composed of shiny, opaque material and was large enough to hold a person. It descended to the platform and stopped next to the Prophet. There was a hissing sound when the capsule created an airtight seal with the chamber below.

The Prophet placed his palm on the dark surface of the cylinder to deactivate the liquid crystal privacy screen and revealed a robed figured standing inside. It was Nancy. Sluggishly, she placed her hand on the inside of the container to mirror his. The Prophet had used drugs to make her compliant and hide her fear so that the congregation only saw engineered serenity.

"Show us the way, acolyte," the Prophet said. "Guide us with your absolute faith."

He raised his hands above his head and backed away from the capsule.

In the chamber below, electric motors whined as the induction coil pivoted to a horizontal orientation and stared up at the sacrifice. A hatch snapped open, and the air inside the capsule shot Nancy into the chamber, through the open portal, and into the Void.

CHAPTER 13

THE WORKING
REHEARSAL

Andi frowned as she stood under the marquee at the Dark Crowd Players theater. She had arrived fifteen minutes early for rehearsal, but Bryan wasn't there. She should have offered him a ride, and he would have been on time.

A bus whooshed past her, and the wave of diesel fumes made her cough. It pulled to a stop at the end of the block, and Bryan stepped off. It didn't take him long to notice her frantically waving.

"You're late," she said when Bryan made it to the theater's entrance.

"I'm ten minutes early," Bryan said and looked down at the ground.

"Come on." Her face tightened as she opened the theater door and went inside.

Alisha was waiting in the lobby.

"Andi, I need some ice." Her chin jutted out until she saw Bryan. "Who is this?"

"This is my... assistant. Don't worry about him, he doesn't say much."

"Assistant?" Alisha said with a confused look on her face.

Bryan stared at the floor and stuck his hands in his pockets.

Alisha circled around him. "Where's my ice? I need it. Bring it to the green room," she said and sauntered off.

Andi let out a long sigh. "Okay, let's go across the street so I can satisfy the queen's thirst." She marched out of the theater with Bryan trailing behind her and jaywalked to the burger joint.

Andi tapped her foot as she waited behind another customer who couldn't decide between fries or onion rings. She wanted to tell the woman that she was taking too long, but before her impatience got the best of her, it was her turn. She ordered two medium drinks, paid, and got her cups.

For the first time, she looked behind the counter through the rectangular pass-through to the kitchen. There was Vance at the grill, literally flipping burgers. He was facing away from her, but the bulging hairnet holding back his red mane made him easy to identify. Andi almost felt some empathy for him, but she remembered it was Vance and got over it. She turned and headed toward the soda machine before he noticed.

"Vance," Bryan called.

Andi squinted down at him and made a crooked frown.

Vance turned to look. His chin dipped when he saw them, but he waved with his spatula. His face was flushed. Andi didn't know if it was because he was standing in front of the grill or embarrassment.

Bryan waved back, but Andi had already reached the drink counter. She filled a cup with ice and Diet Coke and held it out. Bryan rushed over to take it.

"Thanks," he said and proceeded to take a drink.

"Stop! That's for Alisha."

He jerked it away from his mouth so fast it almost spilled. "I thought she just wanted ice."

Andi filled the second cup with ice and held it up as her response.

"Then what's this one for?" Bryan asked.

"Queen Alisha likes to play games. If I return with only a cup of ice, she'll say there aren't any Diet Cokes in the green room. I plan on being ready." She handed Bryan a lid to put on the drink, and the two returned to the theater.

When they reached the green room, the door burst open, almost hitting Andi and spilling the cup of ice she held.

A skinny man dressed like a beatnik exited. It was David, the director, and he eyed Andi for a second before recognizing her. "You quit. Why are you here?"

Andi stepped back. "I needed some time off, but I said I would be here. You must not have heard me."

He made a shooing gesture with both hands and proceeded to the auditorium.

Andi wanted to run after him and ask if she could take part in the rehearsal, but she knew the effort would be fruitless. She led Bryan into the green room and presented the cup of ice to Alisha, who was reclining on the sofa with her feet propped up on a cardboard box.

"I couldn't find any Diet Cokes in the fridge. Can you run and get me one?"

Andi smiled, turned around to Bryan, who was hiding behind her, and took the drink he was holding. "Here you go." She presented the drink like it was a golden chalice.

Alisha smiled bitterly and took the drink. "You should really go straighten up the wardrobe racks. It's a disaster." She slid her feet off the box and stood. As she walked toward the door, she took a sip of the drink and tossed the full cup in the trash on her way out.

Andi grimaced and stepped away from the stream of liquid flowing out of the trashcan's base. She grabbed a roll of paper towels and wadded enough sheets together to absorb the mess. "I guess we'd better check the wardrobe."

Bryan followed her to the room next door.

"Good grief," Andi said. "What do they do in here when I'm not around?" She bent down and started picking up the clothes thrown on the floor.

"I hate to ask this," Bryan said and paused until Andi looked up at him. "I thought you were the understudy?"

"I am, but I have to do all the grunt work to keep my position."

"Has anyone ever mentioned..." He hesitated again. "That you're a totally different person here than you are at Belfore?" He looked down and braced for a lambasting.

Andi had already hung three of the costumes back on the rack and was gathering the pieces for another. "The difference is that here, I really want to do this. At Belfore, I really don't want to be a Voidologist."

"I've only seen two people here, but they're—"

Andi made a dismissive hand gesture. "That's just how artists are. Temperamental. You get used to it."

"If you say so," he said but didn't look at her. "But how are we going to review your High Energy Magnetics in this environment?"

"I studied this afternoon," she said. "Go over the information like you did this morning with Dimensional Physics. I've got the information in my head. I just need your help to understand it." She paused and lowered her voice. "If you tell my father this, I'll deny it, but I think your tutoring was beneficial." She paused again. "Actually, if you tell anyone, I'll deny it."

"You understanding the material was the point." He smiled.

Andi restored the wardrobe room to an orderly state, cleaned the dressing rooms, and finished painting a half-dozen prop swords. While she worked, Bryan reviewed the course fundamentals with her. She could tell that he was amazed by her ability to learn new information in such a short amount of time. She also thought she may have revealed too much of her talent to him, but she didn't have a choice.

It was her secret ability, and nobody else had ever known about it. She sometimes felt that using it to pass her classes was on the verge of cheating, and she didn't want people to think she didn't deserve her three undergraduate degrees. If she were going to get up to speed on her classes and still make rehearsals, Bryan would have to see her talent more than she was comfortable with.

By the time Andi completed her menial tasks, the rehearsal was almost over. She took Bryan to the back row of the auditorium, and the two watched the end of the performance. Alisha played the only female role, Miranda, and was performing the betrothal scene.

Andi leaned over to Bryan and whispered, "She dropped four lines and improvised two others. I've counted twelve variations of her performance in this scene alone, and that's just since we started watching."

Bryan nodded.

She turned to look back at the play but couldn't resist leaning over again. "She's missed so many lines, the play's running seventeen seconds too fast. Ferdinand won't have time to get into position. It's going to be a disaster," she said. "Just wait."

Ferdinand rushed to get into position, tripped, and knocked two other actors over. The scene abruptly ended, and the director jumped up from his seat in the third row and screamed at everyone except Alisha.

Andi looked at Bryan. "I told you."

CHAPTER 14

THE SECOND THOUGHTS

Andi was already awake when her alarm started beeping at 6:00 a.m. She was having second thoughts about spending all the extra time it would require to pull up her grades. What was succeeding in the Voidology program going to buy her? A chance to say, "I told you so?" Was it really worth the effort? She didn't know anymore.

She went along with the whole tutoring thing to keep her father on the rails, but she wasn't fully committed to that path. She had just greased the wheels to buy more time. After a night's sleep, she wanted to blow the whole Voidology thing off, but having the department's existence dependent on her had a certain appeal. There was something about having all that power tingling inside her.

But she had cooled off after her confrontation with Vance. As much as she wanted to shove a passing grade in his face, she wasn't sure she had the desire or the stamina to put in all of those hours. And for what? Perpetuate the biggest dud of a science fair project in history?

No thanks.

All she wanted to do was press the cancel button on her alarm and go back to sleep. She could if she wanted. She had the power. She wouldn't even feel bad if her actions, or lack thereof, cost Belfore its precious grant. Her father was near retirement, and she didn't give a rat's ass about the department's scam to keep its money flowing. She was resourceful, and if she had to, she'd find another way to pay for Juilliard.

Andi sighed at the irony of her situation. With all the effort she put into the theater, she didn't get to act. Her cleaning job was even on shaky ground. She wished that the Dark Crowd Players needed her as much as Belfore did. Maybe she should blow off acting, admit defeat, and move on to something else.

Yes, it was a perfect storm of coincidental circumstances that put her in such a unique position at Belfore. Maybe that was a sign? Perhaps taking advantage of the grant was the right thing to do, and she did want to show all of her doubters just how smart she was.

She deliberated the pros and cons of blowing off Belfore and the theater group for several minutes until it hit her like a slap in the face. Her decision was to delay making a decision. She would simply go down both paths and see how far she could get. If one path became intolerable or blew up, she would focus on the other.

Andi dragged herself to the shower and got ready in record time. She crept down the stairs from her front door, pausing at irregular intervals to see if her nosey neighbor had detected her. She was driving away before Mrs. Nelms cracked her door to investigate.

Andi's High Energy Magnetics class didn't start until ten o'clock, so she could study in the language lab for three hours. She had never crammed so much information into her head in such a short period, but she didn't feel like there was a limit. She just hoped that if she filled her brain to capacity, she hadn't wasted it on a bunch of stupid Voidology trivia instead of a library of scripts.

With two tutoring sessions under her belt, she had a better feel for the kind of information she needed to absorb. She no longer tried to make sense of the data when she listened to it because she knew Bryan would help her string the relevant bits together. With her modified learning strategy, she pulled up the textbook on her tablet and read every word out loud, page after mind-numbing page. She parsed the formulas, dictated the footnotes, and described the figures. When she finished the chapters assigned for her upcoming class, as well as the preceding ones, she unsealed herself from the booth and headed to class. It would have been nice if she could have gone over the information with Bryan before the lecture, but that wasn't an option.

Even with her newfound zeal for learning, Andi thought High Energy Magnetics was still as painfully boring as it was before. It was a cross between watching paint dry and being stuck in traffic, but she had to remain focused. If she didn't pay close attention to every detail Professor Rasmussen said, she would waste time listening to it again, and she couldn't endure that.

She wished that she had paid a little more attention at the start of the semester, but that was water under the bridge. On the plus side, she felt like she was going to be able to grok the information. Catching up on her studies wasn't a hopeless task, just one that would take a lot of her time and a lot of caffeine.

CHAPTER 15

THE UNSCHEDULED EXPERIMENT

After class, Andi needed to find Bryan and set up her next tutoring session. She wanted to get all the High Energy Magnetics information she had queued up in her head converted into a useful form, and she required Bryan to get it there. She had discovered that Bryan and Vance were always in the control room, not just during the exhibitions. She didn't know if it was some kind of bro-cave or if they really needed to be there. Since it saved her a lot of time tracking down her tutor, she really didn't care.

As soon as Andi swung open the door to the control room, she heard the hum of the induction coil charging. "The next exhibition isn't for days. Why are you opening a portal today?" she asked.

"It's for our research," Vance said without turning around. "We get one extra opening a month, and we're kind of busy here." He continued typing at his console.

"Why don't you just do it during the exhibition?"

Bryan turned around to face her. "The more openings, the more information we can gather."

The response puzzled Andi. She believed the Voidology program only opened portals to meet the grant requirements. Nobody was going to discover anything. That's why the rest of the world had abandoned their research into this field years ago. Her eyebrows rose. "What's the experiment?"

"I'm testing my theory that you can detect another portal opening from inside the Void."

Andi cleared her throat. "Whose portal opening are you going to detect?"

"MIT has one scheduled today, and we're overlapping the openings to see if we can detect it."

"Didn't MIT's Voidology program shut down years ago?" Andi asked.

"It did," Bryan said, "but they're heavily invested in exotic material research, and there's nothing more exotic than the superconductors in the induction coil." He smiled.

"Hmm." She had never seen anyone do anything related to the Void that didn't somehow meet a grant requirement. Maybe she hadn't paid close enough attention.

Bryan grabbed a chair at a neighboring console and pulled it next to him. "Come over here, and you can watch."

Andi was curious about their experiment and took the seat she was offered.

"Look here." Bryan pointed to the rows of protocol steps on his computer's display. "The left side shows the procedure for our coil, and the right side is for the one at MIT."

The first five steps of the Belfore side were completed, but only two on the MIT side were.

"We're running one minute ahead of them so we can have our equipment immersed in the Void before they open their portal in Massachusetts."

"Thirty seconds," Vance said.

"The payload has an instrument pack I've been working on for my dissertation. I use shielded wires running out of the Void through the insertion pole, and I'll measure all the signals to see if there's a detectable change when the other portal opens."

"MIT is a long way from here," Andi said. "Are you sure you'll be able to detect something that far away?"

Vance sighed. "If you had been paying attention in any of your classes, you would know there's a consensus among Voidologists that dimensional space inside the Void isn't the same as it is out here."

Bryan turned to him with a scowl on his face. "Andi's worked really hard to catch up, and this is the first glimmer of interest she's shown, so give her a break."

Vance rolled his eyes. He leaned back in his chair. "Ten seconds."

Andi couldn't recall the last time someone had taken up for her like that. She didn't know quite what to think about it. Normally, she would have lit into Vance like an angry hornet and stung him as many times as she could, but she didn't have to do anything this time, thanks to Bryan. It was odd.

"Here we go. Three. Two. One," Vance said.

The wall behind the row of consoles was shared with the test chamber. Being transparent, it provided the best view of the induction coil during a payload insertion. The robotic arm was already moving the pole into position when the portal opening flashed.

"Inserting the payload," Vance said.

Bryan pointed to an area on his screen showing a multi-line graph. "These lines represent the energy levels from fifty sensors placed in the payload. They're pointed in different directions, and each one relays back a signal from inside the Void."

"I thought you couldn't use any electronics in the Void?"

"You can't," Vance said, "but our dude here figured out that you can make a tube from superconducting material and use it to channel energy out of the Void."

"And nobody's tried that before?" she asked.

"I told you, we're doing research," Vance said, but his tone was softer.

"We're coming up on the second portal opening," Bryan said.

All three had their eyes glued to the computer screen. Bryan counted down, "Three. Two. One."

Andi was so caught up in the excitement she was holding her breath along with the other two. The scrolling graphs looked like the seismographs she had seen in movies to detect an earthquake. There were minor fluctuations in some lines, but they were all basically flat as they inched across the screen. When the second portal opened, three of the lines blipped, one more so than the other two. Bryan and Vance jumped up out of their chairs and starting cheering and dancing around.

"I take it that was good?" Andi asked.

Bryan pulled her up out of her chair, and she joined to form a dancing trio.

"It's incredible," Bryan said.

"Epic," Vance said.

The three finally settled, and Vance ran the shutdown sequence on the ring.

Andi was still feeling the shared excitement of the discovery. "What will you do now?"

"I'm going to run all of this by the twins," Bryan said. "Then I'll wait until MIT has another portal opening to confirm my findings."

"How long will that be?"

Bryan frowned. "It could be months."

"That's too bad," she said.

"You almost sound like you're interested in what happens," Bryan said.

Andi looked down, afraid her cheeks were red.

"And one more thing," Bryan said. "There's a truce between you two from now on because we're all on the same team. Okay?"

Vance nodded, and Andi did too.

"Wow," Bryan said. "I'm not sure what the bigger accomplishment was here today."

CHAPTER 16

THE CHANCE

At six o'clock, Andi picked up Bryan in front of the physics building, and she drove them to the theater. They were early, so she thought she would bypass the ritual and went straight to the burger joint before reporting for duty.

"I need three fountain drinks," she said to the cashier. She paid and got the cups.

"Here," she said to Bryan and handed him a cup.

He held it at a distance.

"That's for you. I'll use the other two for Alisha."

"Thanks." He looked into the kitchen to see if Vance was there. "Where's Vance?" he asked the cashier.

The high school kid fiddled with her name badge. "We're not supposed to say anything about it, but I know you guys are his friends." She lowered her voice. "He was late for his shift and got fired."

"Oh, man." Bryan turned to Andi. "He stayed late helping me with my experiment. This is my all fault." He looked down at the floor.

"Why does he have to work at this crappy place, anyway?" she asked.

"His student loans pay for most of his tuition, but he still needs money to live on. He works the late shift at one of those 24-hour breakfast joints too."

"Why doesn't the grant pay his tuition?"

"His parents make too much money."

"And they won't help him out?" Her eyebrows rose.

Bryan shook his head. "They think he's pursuing a worthless degree and won't be able to make a living with it. They have no idea how smart he is."

"Oh," she said and started to understand his visceral reaction to her not-so-nice remarks about Voidology. "Has he asked Rutledge for financial assistance?"

"Many times. You know how Rutledge is."

"Yes, I do." Andi frowned. "Maybe I should talk to my father about it. I could use my leverage with the grant to get him some money."

"That would be great."

"I might not be successful, so don't say anything."

The two got their drinks and crossed the street to the theater. Andi preempted Alisha's beverage request again. The repeated disappointment would probably push Alisha's method of torment in a new direction, but that would be another day.

In the green room, Bryan sat on the sofa and Andi did her cleaning while they reviewed her Dimensional Physics. Ten minutes later, the door swung open, and the director walked in.

"Who is that?" David asked, eyeing Bryan.

"He's helping me study," Andi said.

David brushed his fingertips across his chest as if he was wiping something off his black turtleneck. "You're the understudy, so go do your job."

"Really?" Andi's eyes lit up.

"Jeffrey decided not to show up. You need to recite the lines for Caliban."

"Great!" She dropped the mop back in its bucket and tried to smooth the wrinkles out of her clothes. She turned to Bryan. "Stay here until I get back."

Bryan looked at her with the eyes of a lost puppy, but Andi didn't care. She would show David how good she could be even as the half-monster Caliban. She knew every word the character said. She had a dozen different versions of his performance in her head. She had seen Jeff do it several times. He was adequate, but she could do better. She was going to knock David's socks off.

On stage, Andi was in position. Her first line approached. She was too excited to be nervous. This was the best chance she had ever had to show off her talent. She was Caliban.

"You taught me language, and—"

"Stop. Stop." David was waving his hands so rapidly he looked like he was trying to achieve flight. "Jeffrey has finally graced us with his presence. Go back to your cleaning, Andrea."

Andi's heart sank down to her feet. "It's Andalusia," she said, but nobody heard. She exited stage left and ran back to the green room and slammed the door behind her. Bryan stared at her wide-eyed.

"I didn't even get to show what I could do," she said, and a tear rolled down her cheek.

"What happened?" Bryan asked.

"Jeff showed up right when I was performing my first line."

Bryan paused for a second. "Remember when I gave you advice about Vance, and I was right?"

Andi sniffed and nodded.

"These people treat you like crap, and you're a lot better than they are."

Andi smiled and wiped the tears off her face.

"I don't know if you're a good actor or not, but you're a human. These people don't seem to realize that."

Andi tried to smile. "I want to be an actor, but I can't even show David what I can do. If he said my performance was terrible, I could move on." She lowered her chin.

"I think you should ditch these people and be a Voidologist, but I may be biased."

Andi smiled. "Yes, you are."

"Let me help you finish cleaning, and we can go. You don't need my tutoring, anyway. You caught up faster than I expected." He paused. "That didn't sound very nice. I just thought it would take you, anyone, longer to get a grasp of the information."

"Thanks," she said. "You're a better tutor than I ever imagined you would be."

They laughed. It took them only five minutes to finish the cleaning, and then they left.

CHAPTER 17

THE PROBLEM SOLVER

Andi skipped rehearsals with the Dark Crowd Players for the rest of the week. She hoped David would call and beg her to come back, but that wasn't going to happen. Even if it did, he would try to look up "Andrea's" number. It didn't matter. Andi didn't care about the Players anymore. Well, she did care, but she would intentionally appear not to care, and her acting skills would pull that off.

Missing rehearsals also had a benefit for Andi. It gave her additional time to spend on her studies, and she used it to learn everything she could about Voidology. She also gained some confidence in her knowledge of the subject and no longer felt like a fraud. She didn't have Bryan and Vance's passion for the Void, but she had cultivated a modicum, maybe just a smidgen, of respect for it. At any rate, she no longer believed it was the complete hocus-pocus scam she had always believed it to be. She didn't know when or how, but perhaps one day it would change the world.

It was Monday, again, and the weekly exhibition was about to begin. Andi swung by the control room to confirm the time of her tutoring session. When she opened the control room door, Bryan and Vance were frantically banging out commands on their computers. A siren blared, and there were rows of flashing red lights on every console. The smell of overheated plastic hung in the air, and a popping sound created a frenetic beat. Nobody noticed Andi enter except a lab tech who almost knocked her down running from one console to another. He had already removed several service panels, and another tech was arm-deep in the equipment. A third tech read aloud the emergency shutdown protocol from an old three-ring binder. He flipped the yellowed pages back and forth as if he had missed a step.

"The capacitors will blow if we can't find what's causing the feedback," Vance said. Sweat ran down his face and dripped onto his keyboard.

"I've checked everything," Bryan said. "I can't find anything wrong."

Vance pounded his fists on the console. "It's not accepting my commands."

"Five minutes until it overloads," Bryan said.

A loud pop came from a console, and Andi jumped. A tech brushed by her as he headed to investigate the noise. She moved out of the way and closer to a wall full of metal cabinets housing the high-voltage equipment. Immediately, she noticed an odd hum and put her ear against a louvered access panel. She moved her head back and forth like a bloodhound trailing a scent, except she was after an audible artifact.

To save time during the exhibitions, Vance charged the induction coil to ninety-five percent capacity before Andi started the presentation. That left a couple of minutes for them to capitalize on with the Rutledge effect before the portal opened. Pre-charging the ring was always a simple, uneventful procedure—the complete opposite of the chaos Andi was witnessing.

As the induction coil soaked up power, it generated a natural hum. When it neared the portal-opening threshold, the sound became a low-pitched rumble that could be felt throughout the physics building. Andi had heard it a dozen times, but this time, she sensed that something was off. The sound reminded her of music played out of tune. It was pitchy.

She played back a loop of the sound in her mind and mentally overlaid the audio of a previous run. A sound technician with a high-end audio mixer couldn't have done a better job. After a few seconds of concentration, she smiled and nodded to herself. She knew what the problem was, and nobody else in the control room was even looking in the right direction. She ran over to Bryan. "I know what's wrong."

Bryan was so focused on his console readouts he didn't notice her.

"Bryan," she said in a more urgent tone.

He glanced back at her. "Andi, we're having a crisis."

Vance stood. "We need to evacuate the building. It's going to blow."

"Listen to me!" Andi yelled and stomped her foot.

Bryan, Vance, and the techs all stopped what they were doing and looked at her. "I know what the problem is," she said in a lower tone.

"We don't have time for this," Vance said. "We've got to get out of here."

"Listen to the hum." She held up a finger and started tapping the air. "Don't you hear it? The frequency is off."

Bryan and Vance both shook their heads.

"I think the power inverter failed, and you're getting random spikes in the circuit. The controls won't work because they're caught in a feedback loop," Andi said.

Vance threw her a dismissive look, but then his expression froze as he processed the scenario in his head.

His mouth dropped open.

"I didn't check any of the high-voltage equipment because it's virtually impossible for any of it to fail." He pulled up a diagnostic screen and ran a new series of tests.

It took a tense minute for the test routines to run. The situation in the control room was reaching a critical point, and the anxious techs were about to bug out.

"She's right," Vance said. He banged out some new instructions on his console and ran over to the wall and pulled a large lever to reroute the power flow through a backup. The alarms stopped, and the lights on the consoles all turned green. Vance swiveled his chair to face Andi. "How did you know that?"

"I told you," she said. "It didn't sound right."

"But how did you know it was the power inverter?" Vance asked.

"I wasn't failing all of my classes." She grinned. "I'm acing Superconductor Cymatics."

"But that class is on frequency patterns that initiate a portal opening." Vance blinked rapidly.

"Duh." She snorted. "Frequencies. I took enough undergrad power management classes to know what everything should sound like."

"If I hadn't seen you do it, I wouldn't believe it," he said.

"She's a freak," the lead tech said. "Just like those twins."

Bryan and Vance shot him a reproachful look.

"Oh, poor little tech man's sad because he failed at his job, and the dunce girl made him look like a useless idiot." Andi puckered her face up like a crying baby.

The tech threw the three-ring binder he was holding onto a table and left. His subordinates followed.

"What losers," Andi said.

"I think you totally embarrassed them," Vance said.

"And us too," Bryan added.

"Really, how did you do that?" Vance asked.

"You're welcome," Andi said, ending his line of questioning. "Is the exhibition still on? If not, I'm going back to the language lab."

"Yes." Vance swallowed hard. "I don't see why not."

Andi looked at Bryan. "Are we getting together after the exhibition?"

Bryan nodded.

"Okay," she said. "That's what I came to find out." She pranced to the door, dramatically opened it, and left.

CHAPTER 18

THE NEW TARGET

From his dais in the sanctuary, the Prophet gazed out the dome's faceted windows at the sunlight glinting off the sea of solar panels. Each rectangular module made micro-adjustments to track the sun, giving the appearance of waves rippling across the array. The visual effect had the same relaxing quality as watching the ocean's rhythmic dance. The Prophet used this space to meditate, but more often he thought about the money Belfore paid for the electricity he produced.

The sanctuary dome also provided a buffer between the Prophet and his followers. As a religious leader, he was too much of a distraction to be near the work area. He wanted to have his hands on the research, but working directly with the congregation was incompatible with his role as the Prophet. Inspiration and guidance were the only things he provided them with now.

The suited man approached the steps to the dais. "I have an update."

"About Belfore?" the Prophet asked.

The man nodded. "There's been a development. The new student, the girl, may add value to our research after all."

"What kind of value?" The Prophet raised his eyebrows.

"Details are vague, but our source suggested that the twins are no longer the most valuable target."

The Prophet leaned forward. "Is this girl a savant?"

"She must be something special, or I wouldn't have received the message."

The Prophet stared out the windows again as he pondered the new information. "What's the status of your long-term project?"

"Three more eliminated. There are only two remaining Europeans with talents we can use. If we can't acquire their talent, we'll remove them."

"Good." The Prophet steepled his fingers.

"We should wait a few months before starting in the Americas, or we risk drawing attention," the suited man said.

"We've been eliminating the competition for over a decade. You know I don't enjoy waiting."

"It's time to get our associate involved. We'll need his help to mitigate the girl's recruitment from Belfore."

The Prophet smiled. "Bring her to me."

CHAPTER 19

THE PUZZLE

After another week, Andi's grades continued to improve, and she was almost enthusiastic about being the presenter at the exhibition. She smiled at the audience as she made a rough tally in her head. Before, she had always acted the part, but she had learned so much since then. She appreciated the fact that Bryan, and even Vance, were there as backups for the Q & A, but she thought she could probably handle it on her own. The usher ran down the aisle and handed her the counter. She grinned when she read 123.

The exhibition ran smoothly. Andi knew the performance was her best. As usual, the audience was mostly students. She didn't mind that because they paid the most attention. To top it off, Vance behaved, and there weren't any rude questions from skeptics. So overall, she was having a better-than-average day.

After the last audience member left, Andi proceeded to the control room. Vance was at his computer with Bryan next to him, but there were also two kids she had never seen. She feared they got away from their field trip after the exhibition and someone might be looking for them.

"Hi, Andi," Bryan said. "You did a great job. You didn't even need our help."

"Thanks. That's my job." She rocked back on her heels and smirked, but she felt a little embarrassed at being herself—a first—and she attempted to tone down what she said. "We all know that it's because there weren't any difficult questions. I would never want to do this without your... and Vance's support."

Vance looked away after Andi's almost-compliment caught him off guard.

Bryan smiled. "It's because you understand what you're talking about now, and you might like the program a tiny bit more."

Andi nearly blushed. "We had a hundred and twenty-three attendants. That's up from last week."

Bryan walked over to the two kids. "You said you wanted to meet the twins, so I asked them to stay after the portal opening."

The kids stared at Andi and smiled.

"This is Vernon and Helena," Bryan said.

Andi approached them and bent down. "Hello. It's so nice to meet you." She extended her hand. The two turned to each other and giggled, then they shook her hand together. After they let go, they giggled again and skipped out the door.

"They like you," Bryan said.

"Are you sure?" Andi asked. "They didn't say anything… and they left."

"Trust me." Vance brushed his hair out of his face. "They like you."

"Definitely," Bryan reaffirmed.

Andi puckered her face. "Their actions showed the contrary."

"First," Vance said, "they stayed to meet you. I waited a year before I met them."

"Second," Bryan continued, "they didn't run away crying like they did when I met them."

"Third," Vance said, "they shook your hand. I've never seen them touch anybody but their parents."

"But they're little kids," Andi said. "Why didn't I know that?"

Vance shrugged. "Yeah, they're quirky little dudes, and they don't say much, but never question their abilities. They might as well be a pair of quantum computers on tiny legs."

Bryan grinned. "Their parents are a little overprotective, so they keep a low profile."

Andi wanted to say she didn't believe there was any danger working on a dead project like Voidology, but she wasn't going to taint her new camaraderie. She wasn't sure she still felt that way, either. It was just a habit to always think the worst of it. She also had to admit that it was more pleasant when she wasn't yelling at Vance. They didn't have to be best friends, but they didn't have to butt heads every time they were in the same room either.

"The twins left us a problem," Bryan said. "Do you want to have a go at it?"

She waved her hand. "I don't think I'll be any help."

"It's a puzzle. You listen to a sequence of tones, then you have to draw the pattern it makes to show all the pitch changes. Vance and I can't do it."

"We're tone-deaf," Vance added.

"But I thought you might." Bryan handed Andi a wireless, over-ear headset.

She wasn't sure what the two were up to, but she took one side of the headset and gently pressed it against her ear.

"Concentrate," Bryan said. He held up three fingers, two fingers, one finger, and pointed at Andi. Vance started the playback.

Andi listened for a few seconds. It sounded similar to the old dial-up modems her father used when she was a kid. She thought it was a strange puzzle, but if it came from the twins, maybe that made sense.

She lifted the headphone off her ear and exchanged it with Bryan for a red marker. "And you just want me to draw the pattern?"

Vance and Bryan both nodded.

She went to the whiteboard and drew a wavy line. "There you go."

The other two frowned.

"I told you I wouldn't be able to help." She felt like she let them down.

"I was sure she could do it," Bryan said.

Vance walked over to the whiteboard. He pushed his hair out of his face and picked up a green marker. "Hang on." He drew several line segments through Andi's drawing to create a variable axis. He stared at the whiteboard for several seconds, processing Andi's drawing of the waveform. "I think she got it."

"It doesn't resemble the solution," Bryan said and brought up a graph on his computer.

"Her scale is wonky. If you normalize it on my baselines and view each segment with an independent scale—"

"Wonky? It's not like I had anything to go by."

Bryan paused for a second. "What if we play tones at a regular interval and tell you the frequency of each one?"

Andi shrugged.

"Put the headset back on," Vance demanded.

Andi crossed her arm and pressed her lips together.

Vance realized what he had done. "I'm sorry, Andi. I'm just excited. Will you please try it again?"

She reluctantly put the headset up to one ear. Vance played a range of tones, and Bryan told her the frequency after each increment. Twenty tones later, Andi sat the headset down and stood.

"Don't you need to hear the puzzle again?" Vance asked.

She returned to the whiteboard and sketched a new graph. "How about this one? It's easy to get the scale right when I play it against the reference." She turned to see Vance and Bryan with their mouths hanging open.

"She's got to be playing us," Vance said. "She must have seen the solution."

Andi huffed. "If I were playing you, it would be for something better than this stupid puzzle."

"Can you do another one?" Bryan asked.

"I didn't cheat." She snapped the headphones on both ears and closed her eyes. Vance played a new tone sequence, and Andi drew a perfect representation on the whiteboard. Then he did two more, and she drew two more correct solutions.

"That's incredible," Bryan said.

"I agree," Vance said. "Now, we need to figure out how to insert Andi into the Void."

"Screw that," Andi said. "Are we done?"

"Andi," Vance said. "I want to apologize for every not nice thing I've ever said to you. I was wrong about you. You one hundred percent belong in the Voidology program. I'm sorry I ever doubted you."

Andi looked skeptical. "Whatever."

"Dudes, I have a great idea. My coworkers at the Bull are having a karaoke party," Vance said. "You both need to come. You can be my plus ones."

"Do I have to sing?" Bryan asked.

"Well, of course," Vance said with a serious expression.

Bryan shook his head.

"I'm kidding. You don't have to sing. There'll be plenty of people there willing to make complete fools of themselves."

"What do you say, Andi?" Vance asked.

Andi was at a loss for words. She didn't have to spend time on rehearsals, and she was making progress with her new chosen path. She did enjoy parties, and she was a terrific performer. "Okay."

CHAPTER 20

THE KARAOKE PARTY

Vance's party started at 9:00 p.m. after his shift ended. Andi couldn't believe he spent all day doing research, then worked all night at a restaurant. Until recently, he had two part-time jobs too. She was busy as well, trying to catch up on her studies, but that was different from working to pay for tuition and living expenses. It made her feel a little guilty, but it wouldn't stop her from enjoying the party. Her head was swimming after being in the language lab all afternoon until it closed. She deserved a break, and Vance's party would be a good way to decompress.

Andi found Bryan in the control room as usual. "Can we run through my High Energy Magnetics before karaoke?"

"Sure," Bryan said, "but you don't need my help anymore."

"I'll feel more comfortable if you can go through it with me," she said.

"You know more about the subject than I do."

"I think it just appears that way because I can recall everything, but that doesn't mean I understand all of it."

"You've come a long way since we started."

"Yeah, it's amazing what I can do when I don't have rehearsals to go to. Also, I couldn't have done it without your help. I really appreciate everything you've done to help me, and I realize that I wasn't always the most gracious person."

"Does that mean you plan on finishing your Ph.D.?"

Andi laughed. "Let's not get ahead of ourselves. Besides, my father would have a cow if I told him I wanted to complete my degree after everything I've said to him."

"You're still needed to meet the grant requirements."

She laughed. "At least somebody needs me."

"Now that you're caught up on everything, you can find another theater group."

"Maybe," she said. "I was scraping the bottom of the barrel with the Dark Crowd Players, and I'm sure David has ruined what little reputation I had around here."

The two ran through all the information Andi had absorbed earlier in the day. She wasn't only up to speed; she had passed by most of her classmates.

They left the control room at ten after nine. Andi wanted to be fashionably late to the party, and Bryan didn't care since she was giving him a ride.

"I never asked what the party was for," Andi said.

"It's Vance's birthday," Bryan said.

"Really?" she said. "And here I am without a present."

"It's not that kind of party, and I don't have one either."

"Have you been to one of these parties before?"

"No, but Vance has invited me. Have you ever done karaoke?"

"Yes, I have." She smiled.

Andi parked in front of The Mighty Bull restaurant. Named after Belfore's mascot, it had been a staple amongst students and locals since before the Void's discovery. Through the glass front, they saw Vance behind the counter serving a group of students on barstools. As they walked through the door, he ran around the counter to meet them.

"Dudes, I'm so glad you made it."

"Hey," Andi said. "Where's the party?"

"My replacement's running late, and I've got to cover until he gets here," he said. "Come sit at the counter, and I'll get you something to eat."

Andi and Bryan took a seat, and Vance returned to his station to take their order.

"I want pancakes, bacon, and scrambled eggs," Bryan said without hesitation.

"What about you?" Vance said to Andi.

She hesitated. "Do you have anything vegan?"

Vance frowned. "I don't think so."

"How about a San Pellegrino?"

"Tap water?" Vance asked.

"How about a Coke?"

"Pepsi?" He clenched his teeth.

"Good grief," Andi said jokingly. "Pepsi it is."

Vance poured Andi's drink and handed it to her. He already knew what Bryan wanted and prepared him a vanilla shake. Music blared from a back room.

"It sounds like the party has started without you," Andi said.

"That's okay. We're not missing anything."

"Andi wants to karaoke," Bryan said.

Andi stared at him.

"Is that true?" Vance asked.

"I just said I had done it before, and I can carry a tune better than whoever that pitchy person is singing right now."

Vance laughed. "That's Bob, my manager."

"He's awful," Andi said. "And he should be out here covering for you."

Vance laughed. "It's all good. Bob's the one letting me throw the party." A server brought Bryan's food.

"That was fast," Andi said.

"He always orders the same thing," Vance said. "I placed the order when I saw you drive up."

Bryan shoveled his night-breakfast into his mouth like a starving man.

Andi smiled. "He doesn't get out much."

Vance nodded, but Bryan was too busy scarfing down his food to notice the slight.

"Happy birthday, by the way."

"Thanks," he said.

Two other people at the counter followed Andi's lead and wished Vance a happy birthday too.

Vance stepped away for a minute to take care of his other customers at the counter.

Bryan was fully involved with his pancakes and provided no conversation, so Andi looked around to see who all ate breakfast so late at night. She had never been to the Bull, and she had lived in Belfore her whole life. She wasn't sure why. It looked like a fun place.

When Vance returned, she asked, "Isn't that guy over there the rude tech from the control room?"

"He comes here a lot," Vance said, "but he acts like he's never seen me before."

"Really rude," Andi said with a nod.

"Bryan said you're caught up on your courses. That's remarkable."

Andi pressed her lips together into a frown.

Vance immediately caught his misstep. "Hang on. I meant that as a compliment."

Andi smiled. "Bryan helped. I couldn't have done it without him, and you know," she said and pointed to her ear. "It's kind of like cheating." Her chin dipped.

"I assure you it's not cheating." Vance laughed. "We all wish we could do it."

Bryan nodded as he chewed.

"You're the only person with superpowers I've ever known." He smiled. "It's pretty cool."

"Yeah," Bryan said with his mouth full of food.

"Look." Vance pointed at a guy approaching the door. "There's Larry, my replacement." He untied his apron and threw it under the counter. "Let's go to the party."

Bryan finished cleaning his plate, and the three went to the back room. There were several tables filled with a dozen people. A large-screen TV hung on the wall, scrolling the lyrics of a song. A woman dressed in a staff uniform stood on a short platform opposite the TV and was trying to get up the nerve to sing.

Everyone in the room shouted, "Happy Birthday!"

Vance took a bow. "This is my team of Voidologists in training, Andi and Bryan."

Vance's introduction surprised Andi, but she really did feel like one of the team. She also relieved the poor girl fretting on stage and sang three songs. She never once looked at the lyrics.

"Dude," Vance said when she finished. "I'm blown away."

"You should see me act," Andi said. She couldn't believe she was having such a good time. Then her phone buzzed. She read the message and let out a sigh. "The dean wants me in his office first thing in the morning."

"What did you do now?" Vance said with a grin.

"Who knows?"

CHAPTER 21

THE REPLACEMENT

Andi woke up early the next morning. She couldn't believe how much fun she had at Vance's party. She had always been on her own journey through life, but now, she was part of a team. It felt a little weird, but it was a good weird. She even looked forward to learning more about the Void. Most importantly, she didn't miss the Dark Crowd Players. She thought she might even be excited about the new path she was taking.

Andi's first class wasn't until ten o'clock, so she headed to the dean's office to find out what her father wanted. She had caught up on her classes. She was no longer failing out of school, and the grant was secure. Attendance for the exhibitions was up, and she had saved the induction coil from melting down into a puddle of slag. Maybe her father was going to congratulate her for achieving so much in so little time. She smiled to herself, but then she frowned. He wasn't the type to laud accomplishments, so she psyched herself up for the worst.

"Hi, Andi," the dean's receptionist said.

"Hey, Mary. I was summoned. Can you please let my father know I'm here?" She was about to take a seat in the waiting area, but the dean's door opened, and her father motioned her to come in.

"Andalusia, I've got some good news for you." He smiled.

"Really?" Her tone was full of doubt.

"There's a transfer student from the UK coming to Belfore. He was a doctoral candidate at Cambridge when their program terminated. Voidology has dried up in Europe, and he's been looking for a way to complete his degree."

Andi nodded, not knowing how this kernel of information involved her.

"Belfore accepted him mid-semester and is allowing him to complete his degree here."

She still didn't get where this was going, but she felt the program's dependence on her fading away. "What does that mean for me?"

"It means that you're no longer needed to maintain grant compliance."

Andi had to process what he said for a second before asking, "What about our deal? Are you still going to support me going to Juilliard?"

"You held up your end, and I'll support you going to Juilliard if you get accepted."

"So, I'm just free to go?" she asked in an uncertain tone.

"Yes. The UK student will arrive next week."

"And you don't need me anymore?" She needed to confirm.

"I wasn't expecting to see such disappointment." The dean slid his glasses down and peered over them at his daughter.

Andi grimaced. "Well, I've worked really hard to learn all of this Voidology crap, and now it seems it was all for nothing. I even gave up my position with the Dark Crowd Players."

"Now, you have all the time you need to pursue your other interests," the dean said.

Andi didn't know what to think. She had just lost all of her power. She felt small and useless. She wanted to cry, but she wasn't going to in front of her father. Why did it bother her so much to get dismissed from something she never wanted to be part of in the first place?

"Don't you want to return to your acting?" the dean asked.

"What if I wanted to stay and finish out the semester?" Andi asked.

The dean gave her an incredulous look. "Belfore can't support that many grant participants. You've already asked me to consider Vance McMullen for funding, and I can't support both of you plus a new student."

"I don't want you to cut Vance out." She lowered her head and muttered, "You should have already been funding his tuition."

"I'll let Rutledge and your other professors know you're withdrawing from the program."

"Do I get to keep my apartment?"

"Of course," he said. "You provided the Voidology department with the support they needed in a precarious time, and you deserve something for your sacrifice."

A million things raced through her mind, but the only thing she thought of to say was, "Are you paying my neighbor, Mrs. Nelms, to spy on me?"

The dean laughed. "I'm not paying her, but she volunteers a great deal of information."

Andi scowled. "I knew it."

He shook his head. "I didn't ask her."

"That nosey old lady."

"If it's any consolation, she never told me anything I wasn't already aware of."

"I don't have time to do anything you would disapprove of, anyway."

"Yes, you've been a model student all semester," the dean said sarcastically.

"I am now," Andi said with a hint of pride.

"Yes, I'm very impressed by your progress." He pushed his glasses back up.

"How long will I get to keep my apartment?"

"The lease is for the semester. I'll pay for it until then."

Andi's great day had just turned into a nightmare. She was an idiot for warming up to the idea of being a Voidologist. She should have never wanted to be part of a team whose sole existence relied on grifting a stupid grant. What a fool she had been.

Deviating from her original plan was a mistake. She wanted to be a famous actor, not a Voidologist. If she hadn't made that deal with her father, she would still be with the Dark Crowd Players. She would still be cleaning the green room, but it would be better than her current situation.

Her life was in turmoil, and nobody needed her. She didn't know what to do.

CHAPTER 22

THE THREAT

Andi hadn't left her apartment for three days. She found comfort staying in bed and watching old movies. She had seen them all so many times she didn't even need the sound on. The fictional characters were the perfect guests for her pity party. They didn't ask questions or offer unwanted advice. Facing everyone in the real world was something she couldn't bear. First, she had to figure out what to do with her life.

Bryan had messaged her a dozen times. Her father had apparently told him about the UK student because his messages changed from concern about her not showing up to condolences for losing her position in the program. She even had a message from Vance expressing his sympathies, something she wasn't expecting. She didn't reply to any of them. She would be a ghost for a few more days. What was she going to say? She had worked really hard to save their sorry asses and given up her acting gig only to be thrown out with the trash. It didn't matter that her primary motivation was rubbing her success in the faces of those who doubted her. It also didn't matter that she was selfishly using the grant to pay for Juilliard. She learned all that worthless material and held up her end of the deal with her father.

She considered calling up David and begging for her position back with the Dark Crowd Players. What if she just showed up? She never told anyone she quit. Their first performance was just a couple of days away, and they couldn't have gotten another understudy up to speed.

A head-on approach with David might be too direct, so she grabbed her phone and composed a text to Alisha probing for information. After hovering her thumb above the send button for thirty seconds, she deleted the message. She had burned that bridge and was only asking for more disappointment if she tried to cross it.

On the fourth day, Andi's father messaged her, saying that she needed to attend a meeting in his office immediately. The text started with the word "URGENT" three times in all caps.

When Andi got her first phone in junior high, she and her father agreed that if a text ever started with the attention-getting qualifier, the message could not be ignored for any reason. He had only exercised this privilege once before when her mother died. She was a little shaken just thinking about it, but she didn't know why a meeting would necessitate such seriousness. It was probably some kind of public release from the grant as the new student joined, but she didn't think that would be urgent, not triple urgent anyway. Then a surge of excitement ran through her. They might need her to help with the grant again. Maybe something had happened with the UK student. Maybe he changed his mind, or perhaps he saw Belfore and hopped the next plane back to England. There was a chance, ever so slight, that her bleak prospects were looking up. She had to find out and made it to the dean's office fifteen minutes later, a new record.

Much to Andi's surprise, Dean Fyffe's office was filled to capacity, and she was ostensibly the last of the assortment to arrive. Rutledge was there, as fidgety as ever, along with the department's two faculty members. Bryan and Vance sat in front of the dean's desk. Four campus police officers were standing at attention along with their chief. There were also two people Andi couldn't identify, a tall man with a scar on his forehead and an older woman with a badge hanging around her neck on a ball chain.

The dean walked over to Andi and stared down at her over the top of his glasses. "If I hadn't gotten regular reports from your neighbor, I would have sent the police to escort you over here."

"I'm here. Okay?" Andi leaned away. "But didn't you kick me out of the program earlier this week?" She maneuvered her way to the only empty chair next to Bryan and took a seat.

"This is a serious matter," the dean said.

"Is this about the incident with the power inverter?" Vance asked.

"What incident?" the dean asked and turned to look at Rutledge.

The question caught the department head off guard. "I was going to tell you." He stammered a little. "It was just routine equipment failure, and there was no damage to the coil. The grant covers the replacement cost."

"Then what is this about?" Andi asked. She was tired of the suspense, and she had her life to plan.

The dean took in a breath. "These FBI agents have brought to our attention," he said, motioning toward the two out-of-place individuals, "that someone may be trying to harm those involved with Void research."

"What?" Andi's laughed. "Aren't we the only ones involved with this fruitless endeavor?" She almost regretted saying that, but she no longer had any affiliation with the program, so she should be able to speak poorly about it if she wanted. If they could ditch her, she could abandon them.

The man with the scar cleared his throat. "I'm Special Agent Michael Hayden with the FBI." He pulled open his suit jacket to reveal a badge clipped to his belt. "We've received intel from Interpol that has some alarming implications." He pressed his lips together as he let his announcement sink in. "Last week, three faculty members in France died in a lab accident. The local authorities determined it was sabotage, and the investigation expanded, turning up twelve other incidents involving students or faculty. The deaths all appeared to be accidental or from natural causes. They occurred in several countries, and the first death was seven years ago. However, there was a common denominator. Everyone had been involved in Void research at one point in their career."

Rutledge interrupted. "We've had a hard time finding students for our program. Is somebody trying to sabotage the grant?"

"I think you're jumping the gun," Hayden said. "None of the deaths have been in the US, and there's no specific threat directed toward Belfore. However, this is the only active Void research facility left, so we have a responsibility to oversee your protection until we can determine what's going on."

"Who'd want to kill Voidologists?" Andi blurted out, and her father squinted at her.

The female agent stepped closer to Andi. "There are several factions who vehemently oppose Void research, fearing it will cause the end of the world. Then on the other end of the spectrum, there are those who worship it, like a religion."

"Agent McKenzie specializes in cultic studies and is an expert on the Rutties," Hayden said.

Rutledge grimaced.

"No offense, Dr. Rutledge, but that is what they're called."

Andi took a little pleasure in watching Rutledge's expression tighten from his discomfort, and she thought she would get some revenge and turn the screw a little more. "Why are they called Rutties?"

McKenzie was eager to respond. "It's a derogatory moniker derived from Jonathan Rutledge's name. He discovered the Void and was the first one to enter it."

Andi laughed and turned to Rutledge. "You could be their leader." If they wanted a stressed-out accountant who wasn't very accomplished or charismatic, she thought.

Rutledge scowled.

"These Rutties are crazy enough to kill people?" Andi asked.

"It's a cult, and they don't play by the rules," the agent said. "They're trying to reach God, and they don't care what they do to get there."

Hayden moved closer to the dean. "We should also investigate the recent equipment failure. We need to rule out foul play."

"I don't think it was anything intentional," Vance said. "It's just a twenty-five-year-old inverter that wore out."

"It won't hurt to be thorough," Hayden said. "We'll get a forensic team to inspect it."

The dean nodded and looked at the students. "The FBI will provide protection for everyone in the department. The twins' parents have opted to get private security against my advice. But the—"

Hayden interrupted. "The rest of you won't have that option. I've assigned agents to monitor the other faculty members. Dr. Rutledge, being the department head and also the son of Jonathan Rutledge, is at a higher risk than the other faculty members. He'll need to be sequestered with the students."

"I will be more comfortable in my own home," Rutledge said. "I won't let some cult intimidate me."

"That's your choice, but I'll be posting agents outside your residence."

Andi raised her hand to stop the briefing. "What exactly do you mean by sequestered?"

"We're commandeering an empty floor in one of the dormitories and will keep the three of you there for enhanced security."

"First, let's be clear that I'm no longer part of this program since my father threw me out last Monday. I was never really in it, and I didn't contribute anything to it, so I don't think some crazy cult will be interested in me. Second, I have no desire to hold up in some filthy dorm for an unknown duration."

Hayden shook his head. "We can't count on a cult being abreast of your current status. And I'm sorry, Miss Fyffe, but your protection is not optional."

Andi wasn't giving up. "Okay, then let's try this from a different angle. The program hasn't had a great deal of success. Even a cult would know that. Are you sure we're actually at risk?" She didn't want to be stuck in a dorm for any amount of time, even if it meant dissing Bryan and Vance's accomplishments.

"We can't take any chances," the dean said. "The FBI is here to make sure we don't."

"Isn't my nosey downstairs neighbor enough protection?" Andi asked. "I bet she'll inform you of what's going on before the FBI could."

"I don't think you're taking this threat seriously. People have been murdered for tangential associations with Void research, and this program is the center of it all," Hayden said.

Andi wasn't concerned about her safety in the least. She worried about how this inconvenience would interfere with her life. How was she going to figure out what to do next while locked in a dorm room?

CHAPTER 23

THE SEQUESTRATION

"I can't believe we're trapped in this disgusting place," Andi said, scanning the dorm's common area where the FBI had deposited the three students. "A four-star hotel would have been just fine."

Vance shook his head. "This place is a lot nicer than the dump I live in." He plopped on a vinyl sofa and kicked his feet up on a well-worn coffee table. "We've each got our own room. I've never had a room of my own, ever. This is Shangri-La."

Andi grimaced. "You have a strange idea of paradise." Her eyes followed a dark stain across the threadbare carpet until it disappeared under a wall.

"Hey, I live in this dorm," Bryan said. "My room's three floors down."

"Dude, you've made a lateral move." Vance laughed. He made a side-to-side motion with his hand and then changed it to an up-and-down motion.

Bryan shrugged.

Andi crossed her arms. "I feel sorry for both of you."

"If we can't leave this floor, does that mean they're bringing food?" Vance asked. He licked his lips in anticipation.

"It'll be slop from that cafeteria downstairs," Andi said. "I smelled it as soon as we entered the building."

"I like the food here," Bryan said.

Andi wrinkled up her face. "The aroma reminded me of my grandmother's nursing home."

Bryan turned to Vance. "It's not that bad."

"I can't wait to try it." Vance rubbed his belly.

Andi wanted to belittle her new prison some more, but she remembered something else. "*The Tempest* opens tonight. I was going to disguise myself and sit in the back row." Her tone was full of self-pity.

"You're better off not worrying about that," Vance said. "Even if you could go, that crazy cult might get you."

"You're kidding, right?" Andi asked. "You're the one who made a breakthrough in Void propulsion. A cult isn't going to expend their energy on me. I don't know anything. You, on the other hand..." She smiled. "Or even Mr. I-Can-Detect-Another-Portal-Opening-At-A-Distance." She looked at Bryan.

"They won't be interested in me," Bryan said. "But they should be interested in you."

"Why is that?" She tilted her head to the side in anticipation of the fantasy she was about to hear.

"If the twins can analyze the background radiation in the Void, they would have enough information to complete their work. All we need to do is get you inside the Void so you can listen to a resonator. Your ability to remember what you hear makes you valuable to anyone researching the Void."

"Thanks for pointing that out," she said sarcastically. "And please don't inform the crazy cult of the remote possibility of me being able to help them find God. Besides, I can't analyze background radiation. You would be misleading them."

"You can record waveform information better than high-end electronics. All the twins need is a clean reading from inside the Void."

Vance had been pondering Bryan's proposal. "The probe I built for my full-scale propulsion test has enough space for you, Andi. Do you want to go for a ride?"

Andi snorted. "So it can rip my flesh off while my blood boils, and every cell in my body gets its DNA shredded?" She shook her head. "Thanks, but no thanks."

"If you had the appropriate shielding," Bryan said, "it would work."

"My probe is rated for a vacuum," Vance persisted.

"I'm not going in the Void, so just get that ludicrous thought out of your heads."

"Bryan's right," Vance said. "It'd work."

"And you would get rid of me too? What happened to being a team?"

"We don't want to get rid of you," Bryan said.

"Especially since we need you alive to bring back the information," Vance said and laughed. "If you die in the Void, this plan wouldn't work."

"Why don't you use those shielded tubes like you used in your experiments?" she asked.

"I've tried, but the translation out of the Void scrambles the data," Bryan said. "But if you were inside, you could listen to the receiver with no distortion."

"If electronics won't work, what would I listen to?"

Vance jumped up. "Several years back, one of the European groups invented a device that generates a sound based on the frequency and amplitude of electromagnetic radiation in the Void. It's mechanical with no electronic parts."

"Then hook it up to old-fashioned paper tape and let it draw you a graph," Andi said.

"The device is like a divining rod. You have to hold it just right and feel when it's in the right spot to get a reading. It's too difficult to use autonomously without any electronics."

"Then how do you know it even works?"

"They work even if you place one outside an open portal, but the data is distorted."

Andi shook her head. "I'm still not seeing how I can help there."

Bryan looked down at the floor. "We have a confession to make. Remember the puzzles you solved? We were testing you."

"Good grief," she said. "You two need to grow up. If you wanted my help, you should have just asked."

"You would have said no," Vance said.

"Absolutely." Andi leaned back in her chair.

"I'm going to say this, and you won't believe it's coming from me," Vance said, "but what you can do is freaking awesome. You might win the Nobel Prize."

"Ha ha," she said. "That's funny."

"Actually," Bryan said, "the twins would win, but you would get some credit."

Andi thought about winning a Nobel Prize. It piqued her interest. Honestly, she would rather have an Oscar, but an award is an award. "How can drawing a waveform help the twins?"

Vance leaned closer to Andi. "We know how physics in our reality works, but our observations show that the Void is different. Our physics and Void physics both use a similar set of equations, but the constants are totally different, and we don't know the values for the Void. The difficulty for the twins is that there are too many unknown variables to solve their equations. It doesn't matter how smart they are if they don't have enough information to do the math."

"And you're the key," Bryan said.

"Exactly," Vance said. "You can listen to a resonator in the Void and draw a perfect waveform. That information would allow the twins to complete their equations. It would be like Penzias and Wilson discovering cosmic background radiation in the sixties."

Andi nodded her head to show that she understood, but she didn't. "Did they win a Nobel Prize?"

"Yes," Bryan and Vance said at the same time.

Andi shook her head. "It doesn't matter. You aren't sticking me in the Void. There's no way to keep it from killing me, so your wonderful idea is really not that wonderful."

"Ten years ago," Vance said, "there was a prodigy here at Belfore. Her name was something Dillinger, as in the Dillinger proposition for electron migration in the Void."

"Nancy," Bryan said.

"Yeah, Nancy Dillinger. She was leading the research into shielding technology for the Void, but she dropped out before completing her dissertation. If we can get the twins to pick up her work, we might have viable shielding before the end of the semester." He smiled.

"I'm not even in the program anymore, so it doesn't matter," Andi said.

"Yeah, Bryan and I don't understand that. Even if the program gets a new student, you shouldn't have to leave."

Andi shrugged. She wasn't going to tell them she had negotiated Vance's funding with her father. Her phone buzzed just in time to end their discussion.

As she read the message, a grin stretched across her face. "Alisha has food poisoning!"

"Whose Alisha?" Vance asked. "And why does her unfortunate choice of cuisine make you so happy?"

"She's from the theater, and she's Andi's nemesis," Bryan answered.

"I thought I was her nemesis," Vance said with a smile.

"You're not in the same league as Alisha."

Andi was beaming. "She can't perform on opening night. David is begging me to come fill in for her. He even got my name right. My wish has come true."

"I hate to rain on your parade," Vance said, "but you won't be able to get out of here with the FBI watching."

Andi rubbed her chin. "What will it cost me to get your help?"

CHAPTER 24

THE OPPORTUNITY

"We have a recruitment opportunity tonight in Belfore," the suited man said.

"The dean's daughter?" the Prophet asked. He had done some research on Andi.

The suited man nodded. "She possesses a talent we do not have in the congregation."

"From what I understand, she's flunking out of school. How could she possibly be of use to me?"

The suited man smiled. "Her unique ability is something we alone can exploit, and it has nothing to do with her academic prowess."

"Is she more valuable than those wonder twins?"

"Probably not, but they're unrecruitable. The girl is our next best option."

"Is she going to be receptive to our special environment?"

"Apparently, she's not receptive to anything."

"We know how to handle the uncooperative." The Prophet smirked. "And I enjoy challenges."

The suited man snorted. "I think you enjoy playing cult leader too much, and your obsession is interfering with our goals."

"Our goal is to restore credit where it properly belongs." The Prophet scowled. "Our goal is to punish Belfore for its crimes." His volume increased. "Our goal is to control the Void." He was shouting before he finished.

The suited man had no reaction to the rebuke other than to state, "My goal is to make an insane amount of money."

"Controlling the technology related to the Void will reap all the riches you can imagine."

"I'm counting on that," the suited man said.

The Prophet didn't care about money, only revenge.

CHAPTER 25

THE KIDNAPPING

I'm going to my prison cell," Andi said to Bryan and Vance as she headed to her dorm room. She was just loud enough for the FBI agents to hear, but not loud enough to be suspicious. She was an actor, and she knew the exact number of decibels to use.

Bryan had told Andi about a maintenance shaft at the end of the hallway. Residents called it the Love Tunnel, and an entrance was hidden on each floor. The daring used it to sneak unauthorized guests in and out of the dormitory. The shaft was only two-foot square, but it was large enough to crawl through and led to a service area in the bowels of the building where a ladder descended to the ground floor.

Bryan and Vance agreed to improvise a distraction at 7:00 p.m. in exchange for Andi considering a trip into the Void if, and only if, they proved it was completely safe. She didn't expect that to happen in her lifetime. At the arranged time, she cracked her door open to the sound of hooting and hollering; it was football-related. All the agents were engaged in the banter, giving her an opportunity. She made her way to the end of the hallway and slipped unnoticed into the shaft.

The Love Tunnel was dark and dirty, and she had to use the flashlight on her phone to see where she was going. She half expected to find the corpse of an unfortunate freshman who fell off the ladder and plunged to their death, but not even that would have stopped her from making the performance.

Andi emerged from a panel in the wall near the building's rear entrance. There were a couple of students who saw her exit, but they didn't give her a second look. How could a girl crawling out of a secret hatch garner so little attention? What kind of dorm was this, and how was Bryan privy to this *feature*? She had many questions, but no time to ponder them.

Bryan had also loaned Andi the bus pass he wore around his neck on a lanyard and briefed her on using public transportation. It was an alien concept to Andi, but she couldn't use her car without drawing attention. She made it downtown in forty-five minutes. It would have taken only five if she had driven herself, but she got there without setting off any alarms.

She spotted David through the glass façade of the theater as she trudged up the hill from the bus stop. He checked his phone and paced back and forth like he might bolt from his crumbling production. Andi savored him having to sweat over it.

"Where have you been?" he yelled as soon as she opened the door. "This production doesn't revolve around you, sweetie."

"I had to ditch the FB—"

He waved his hands to silence her. "I don't care about your issues. Get that cleaning girl, Angela, to help with your costume."

Andi nodded. "I'll do that." She wanted to verbally assault him. An opportunity like this would never happen again, but she stopped herself. Instead, she would give him a performance so spectacular that he would have to take her acting skills seriously. Alisha's unfortunate event was her ticket back into the theater group, and she couldn't have planned these circumstances better if she had tried.

"And don't mess this up, or I'll ban you from the industry." David stretched his turtleneck and walked away.

Andi didn't think he was quite that influential, but she suppressed her desire to correct him and headed to the wardrobe room. Her character, Miranda, wore a vintage blue dress, but she couldn't find it on the racks. She swiped through the clothes at a frantic pace, but there was no blue dress. After several more passes through the costumes, she finally let out a sigh and gave up looking for it. Alisha must have taken it with her. Besides a pirate uniform, the only costume close to her size was a frilly dress. It was bright red and more can-can than Elizabethan, but she would make it work. *The Tempest* was a fantasy; her costume didn't have to be period-accurate. If David had a meltdown, she would blame "Angela."

Andi had watched Alisha do her makeup a dozen times. All she did was exaggerate her features with hard lines, and Andi thought she had mimicked the look pretty well. She was brushing her hair one final time when she heard the door open.

"I'm almost ready. Give me a sec." She braced for a caustic reply from David.

When he didn't respond, she turned to see who it was, and a man dressed in black grabbed her head and pressed a cloth over her face. She smelled something sweet before blacking out.

CHAPTER 26

THE PROPHET

Andi came to with a sneeze. The frills of her dress had flipped up onto her face and tickled the inside of her nose. All she could see was light diffused through the red dress. Her head throbbed, and her tongue stuck to the roof of her dry mouth. The sound of approaching steps startled her, and she fought the frills off her face. She found herself high above the floor on a clear acrylic platform in a large, circular room. There were no identifying marks other than four gold circles spaced around the wall's perimeter, and she didn't know what they represented. She scooted over to the edge, and her stomach dropped when she saw the floor was at least fifteen feet below.

"Greetings, Miss Fyffe," a voice said in a not-so-friendly tone.

The acoustics of the round room were such that Andi couldn't tell where the voice came from. She spun herself around on the slick surface until she glimpsed a middle-aged man standing at the base of the platform wearing an ornate, white robe. She thought he looked like a cosplayer dressed as some kind of wizard. He just needed a big pointy hat.

"Who are you?" she asked.

"I am the Prophet," he said.

"Good grief," Andi said. "The prophet of what?"

"The Church of the Void," he said in a confident tone.

"What?" She wasn't sure she heard him right. "Why have you brought me here?"

"You, my dear, are the congregation's newest recruit."

She narrowed her eyes as she stared down at him from her elevated perch. "I hate to break it to you, but there's been a mistake."

"I am just as surprised by your usefulness as you are."

Andi looked for a way off the platform. "You ruined my performance. They'll never let me back in now."

"It's time for you to live up to your potential and stop wasting your talents."

"You have no idea what my talents are." Andi had reached her limit with the man.

"I do, Miss Fyffe, and I have a much more important task for you than performing in a silly play."

"Like what?" She cocked her head to the side.

"My destiny." His tone was full of conceit. "You will restore my proper place in history."

Andi gave him a puzzled look. "Can you tell me again exactly who you are?"

"I opened the doorway to God, and you will help lead my congregation through it."

"You're crazy." Andi laughed. "And Grandpa, you need to work on your appearance. Nobody's going to take you seriously in that gaudy bathrobe."

The Prophet laughed. "You're not one to judge the appropriateness of another's attire." He nodded toward her.

"I was in a play, you moron." She beat back the red frills again. "What's your excuse?"

The Prophet didn't respond.

Andi scooted around the platform, looking off the edge. "How do I get down from here?" Andi took off her red shoes and threw them at the Prophet. He moved out of the way to avoid getting hit.

When he looked back at her, she hung off the edge of the platform about to let go.

"Security!" the Prophet shouted.

Andi dropped to the floor in a blur of red frills and rolled to absorb the impact. The Prophet backed away from her, obviously not accustomed to his captives confronting him. Three guards rushed in front of her.

"You're one of those Rutties, aren't you?" she said.

The Prophet scowled. "That name gives credence to the false prophet."

Andi snickered. "I'll take that as a yes."

The Prophet's face turned as red as Andi's dress. "You know nothing, child." He motioned to the guards. "Prepare her for communion."

"What's communion?" Andi asked.

CHAPTER 27

THE PLUNGE

Security guards escorted Andi to an elevator outside the communion hall. They rode up several floors and proceeded down a hallway to a small staging room where two robed attendants waited. One was an older woman, shorter than Andi. Her once black hair was mostly gray, and Andi thought she looked familiar. The other attendant was a teenager. She was tall and skinny with a freckled face. The two didn't speak as they stripped off Andi's frilly dress leaving her almost naked in front of her abductors.

The older attendant pulled a gray jumpsuit from a storage locker and held it up next to Andi. She adjusted several straps and unfastened several Velcro pieces before handing it to the captive.

"You've got to be kidding," Andi said, but she took it.

"You've got two minutes to get it on," a guard said, leering at her.

He made Andi uncomfortable as she stood there in her underwear, so she sat on a bench and started donning her new attire. If nothing else, the perv would have less to look at. She pushed her feet into the strange suit's legs and wriggled it up and over her shoulders. It reminded her of a wetsuit, only thicker and less stretchy. She pushed her hands into the sleeves, but the suit was too large for her fingers to reach the gloved ends. The inside lining felt like latex, but the exterior was a flexible wire mesh.

The senior attendant pulled up an industrial-grade zipper closing the front of the suit. The younger one cinched several leather straps on her arms, legs, and back. The jumpsuit had a steampunk quality with its brass buckles and hoses, even though it was obviously an advanced piece of technology. Andi was surprised by how well it conformed to her frame after the adjustments. It was even comfortable until the older attendant stretched the suit's hood over her head and wrapped several flaps around her neck and chin.

"Hold your breath," the younger attendant said, picking up an oval-shaped, convex lens.

Andi gasped right before the girl pressed the final piece into place over her face, sealing the suit.

When she couldn't hold in the air any longer, she blew it out and fogged up the transparent faceplate. When she tried to inhale, there was nothing. She strained to pull air into her lungs, but her diaphragm was stuck. She was suffocating. When she tried to claw at the faceplate, the guards restrained her. The sound of her heart drummed so loudly that she couldn't hear what the attendant was saying, and she only saw shadows through the condensation. As she struggled to get loose, the lights grew dim. She was losing consciousness.

A metallic click followed by a hiss interrupted Andi's asphyxiation. A cool breeze blew across her face, and she sucked air in as quickly as her lungs would expand. The faceplate cleared, and she saw that one of the attendants had connected a canister of air to the suit. It was no larger than a can of Coke.

The older attendant hung a rectangular device, about the size of a school lunch box, on a hook at the front of Andi's waist. Its heft pulled her off balance, but she adjusted her stance to compensate. The attendant grabbed a thick electrical cable dangling on the side of the jumpsuit and plugged it into the box. Andi felt the hairs on the back of her neck stand up, and she didn't think it was from fear.

A circular door in the staging room's ceiling retracted with a clank, and a transparent container lowered out of the opening. It was cylinder-shaped, over six feet tall, and hung on the end of a pole. It looked like a larger version of the payload apparatus used in the weekly exhibitions, except it operated in a vertical orientation. When it reached the floor next to Andi, the younger attendant inserted a stainless-steel implement into several latches, and the front half of the container swung open like a large clamshell.

Two of the guards pushed Andi into the container and closed her inside.

She banged on the inside and screamed as the attendant locked the latches with the metal tool.

"Keep shouting," a guard said. "You'll use up all of your air."

Andi stopped resisting and tried to calm herself. She didn't believe the tiny canister had much air, and she didn't know how long they would imprison her in the suit. She took a slow, deep breath and concentrated on her breathing. It was a meditation technique she always used before a performance. It was working until a door in the floor opened. The container jolted as it began lowering—with her inside—through the floor.

Andi descended into the communion hall. The circular, white wall contrasted with the black floor. The odd, translucent platform marked its center, and four gold circles were evenly spaced around the circumference. From her perspective, it looked like a giant compass rose.

The Prophet stood on the platform and stared up at Andi descending into the hall. She saw his smug expression, but something more alarming caught her attention. He wasn't on top of some weird pulpit. It was a test chamber, just like the one at Belfore. Through the transparent platform, she saw an induction coil looking up at her. How had she missed that detail when she crawled off the platform before? And how could a crazy cult have an induction coil?

When the container came to a rest next to the Prophet, he placed his hands on its surface in ceremonial fashion. "Are you enjoying your communion?"

Andi heard him through the suit's com system, but she didn't answer.

"Few experience communion so early in their tenure. Even then, I only choose those who have contributed greatly to the Church."

His arrogant grin was nauseating, and it didn't help Andi's already maxed-out stress level.

From the base of the chamber, an overweight man wearing a suit shouted, "Cut out the dramatics and get on with the test."

Besides the Prophet, he was the only other person Andi could see in the hall.

"He takes the fun out of everything," the Prophet said and winked at her.

The induction coil beneath her began emitting the Rutledge effect. With her capsule positioned directly above the ring, there was no doubt what they had planned.

It terrified her.

The Prophet tapped on the cylinder to get Andi's attention. "We have equipped your suit with two harmonic resonators." He mimed, twisting something on the side of his head.

Andi reached up and touched three knobs of different sizes on each side of the suit's hood.

"You must tune the equipment to get a reading, and you'll only have until the portal closes."

She jumped when a hatch opened beneath the container.

"Make sure you use that gift of yours. If you don't bring something useful back to me, your next communion will be a one-way trip." He rapped on the cylinder with his fist three times, and the pole suspending the container from the hall's ceiling started lowering it into the chamber.

Andi wanted to scream but didn't want to use up her tiny can of air.

When her container stopped lowering, it hovered a few inches above the horizontally oriented induction coil. A seal inflated around the pole where it entered the test chamber, and a hissing sound permeated the capsule. It was the same noise generated by the pumps evacuating the air out of the test chamber at Belfore.

When the Rutledge effect became bright enough to reflect off the interior of the chamber, the dancing lights projected onto the curved wall of the communion hall. It was beautiful. Andi could have stared at the spectacle for hours, and she was right about its hypnotic rhythm being perfect for a disco.

When the portal opening flashed, she jumped again. She tried to rub her eyes, but the faceplate was in the way.

With no warning, the pole attached to the top of the container telescoped out and pushed Andi into the Void. She believed she was about to die.

The transition into the Void was smooth and uneventful. She didn't sense any change other than the light growing dim. Then something yanked the rug from under her feet. She was weightless and falling—or floating, she couldn't tell which.

She paddled her arms around like she was in a swimming pool, but it had little effect. The lack of gravity and her unnatural movements made her nauseous. Just the thought of vomiting in the suit raised her anxiety level another notch, so she closed her eyes and concentrated on not being sick.

When she felt more in control of her stomach, she opened her eyes and found that being in the Void was ethereal. She didn't know if the sensation was from the weightlessness or the complete detachment from reality. She understood how someone might perceive this so-called communion as a religious experience, and it didn't take a brainwashed cult member to appreciate it.

Andi assumed she wasn't going to die—immediately, anyway. So, she reached up to the left side of her head and rolled the largest knob between her fingers. She heard nothing at first, so she tried again more slowly until there was a blip of static. Like tuning in a station on an old analog radio, she found a staticky area and tried to clear up the signal with tiny adjustments. When she couldn't improve the signal anymore, she switched to the medium-sized knob, which made more precise adjustments. The random static became harmonized. The smallest knob got her to a frequency modulation reminiscent of the twin's puzzle she solved for Bryan and Vance. She repeated the process with the second set of knobs and ended up with a multi-layered hum playing in stereo.

Andi's eyes adjusted to the darkness allowing her to see a faint red glow all around her. It undulated as if there were ripples distorting her view. She had always thought it was completely dark and empty in the Void, hence its name. But it wasn't, and it was beautiful. She guessed that only the Rutties knew this. She looked up at the point of light where she entered. It looked like a twinkling star showing the way out.

Her container jolted again when it stopped moving. She had less than two minutes left in the Void and positioned herself to float in the middle of the cylinder. She folded her legs into the lotus position and tried to relax. Pinching her thumbs and forefingers, she closed her eyes and listened to the complex array of sounds. The information density was far greater than anything she had tried to absorb before. There were dozens of bands to process, and strange patterns filled the data stream. It was too complex and nuanced. She didn't believe she would be able to absorb anything useful, but she had to. It was the only thing she could bargain with.

Andi took in a deep breath. Forcing her doubts aside, she focused on the sound coming out of the resonators. It took a few seconds to get a sense of what she needed to do, but she was doing it. She filled herself with the song of the Void and felt confident in her abilities. She started to see the waveforms take shape in her mind, then her air ran out.

The air blowing on her face stopped. The canister was empty. It only took a second before she struggled to breathe. Her heart raced as she strained to suck in more air, but there was none.

The container lurched as the pole pulled it back toward the pinpoint of light at the exit. Andi bounced around the container like a pinball in the weightlessness. Her mind slowed down as her oxygen-starved body gave up. She was losing consciousness when bright lights forced her to squeeze her eyes shut. Gravity reasserted itself and slammed her to the floor of the container where she finally passed out.

CHAPTER 28

THE WAVEFORM

The throbbing in Andi's head snapped her back into consciousness. She was supine on the bottom level of a bunk bed. Someone had replaced her Void suit with a long white robe. It wasn't ornate like the Prophet's, and it would have passed for a bathrobe if not for its hood. She figured her new attire was the Prophet's punishment for her previous remarks about his. But the robe was a lot more comfortable than the frilly dress and the weird scuba suit.

She was on the corner bunk closest to the door, but the room had at least a hundred perfectly made beds. There were no windows. The room's walls were white. The floors and the ceiling were white. Everything was white. The only color was a red light on top of a numeric keypad next to the only door.

Andi stood too quickly and became dizzy. Her head hurt even worse in an upright position. She shuffled toward the door but had to stop and rest. Her head started spinning, and she couldn't stop herself from falling face down onto the floor. It was an undignified position, but the cool tiles felt soothing on her face, so she decided to rest there for a minute. She prepared herself for a second attempt, but she heard someone outside the door keying in a code. The door clicked and swung open.

The Prophet entered, followed by the suited man and three security guards. He stared down at Andi sprawled on the floor. "Miss Fyffe, it's so nice of you to rejoin us, but I must say, you've looked better."

"Uh-huh," she mumbled. She knew she was not at the top of her game because that was the best comeback she could muster.

The guards picked her up and sat her on the closest bed.

"We've come to see what you can do for me," the Prophet said. His hair looked grayer up-close, and there were crow's feet around his eyes. He was taller and thinner than the suited man, but they were similarly aged.

Andi pressed on her temple with two of her fingers and squeezed her eyes shut. "Can you get me a glass of water and something for this headache?"

"I'm sure we can find something," the Prophet said. "But you must first prove your usefulness."

She kept her eyes closed. "And what exactly do you think I can do for you?"

"We don't have time for games, Miss Fyffe."

She opened her eyes and stared up at him. "What do you want?" Her tone was as sharp as the pain piercing her skull.

"You will convey all the information you recorded in that pretty little head of yours."

She took in a deep breath and exhaled. "It was just a bunch of static. It sounded like this." She made a crackly sound with her mouth.

He shook his head. "We have informants at Belfore. We know what you're capable of."

"Then I'm sure you also know that I'm no longer in the Voidology program at Belfore, and even when I was, I was failing."

"We're aware of your dismal academic performance," he said, "but I'm not interested in your scientific knowledge."

"That's good because I wouldn't be able to help you there."

"My congregation has the best Voidologists in the world. There is nothing Belfore's disgraced program could contribute."

"Are your Rutties smarter than the twins?" Andi felt better and couldn't resist just one gibe.

The Prophet pressed his lips to form a fine line but didn't respond.

"Perhaps," Andi said and wobbled her head, "you should have kidnapped them and shoved them through your big metal donut."

The Prophet scowled at Andi's choice of words. "Take her to the chapel." He turned around and headed for the door.

Andi recognized something familiar in the Prophet. He had the same visceral reaction as Vance when she dissed the ring. But if he was really trying to understand the Void, what was with the crazy cult? It made no sense to her. She also thought she recognized his voice, but she wasn't sure.

The guards escorted Andi to the chapel. She didn't know why it was called that because it didn't resemble a chapel or any part of a church she had ever seen. Concentric rings of workstations filled the room, and a robed person manned each of the high-end computers. It was a research facility, and it was much more impressive than Belfore's. Billboard-sized screens hung from the walls giving the look of mission control for a space launch. Graphs and data scrolled by on several, another showed a view of the induction coil in the communion hall, and another showed a view of the chapel.

Everyone there stared at Andi with awe. Some bit their lips, others had jittery feet, but all were silent. She wondered why they were so anxious to see what she brought back. One of the observers pulled a marker out of his robe pocket and handed it to her. Two portable whiteboards were rolled against the wall closest to her.

"Draw the waveforms produced by the resonators," the Prophet commanded.

Andi's face tightened just at the sound of his voice, but she wouldn't let him intimidate her. "I don't think you understand how this works," she said. "Yes, I heard a hum in there, but drawing whatever you want is unrealistic."

"I know you're capable of rendering the structure of complex signals just by listening to them." He flipped over his tablet and showed the various graphs she had produced for Bryan and Vance.

"Yeah, I did that stupid puzzle. I didn't get it right the first time, and I certainly didn't know what I was doing. Besides, what I heard in the Void is way beyond that simple stuff." She waved a dismissive hand at him, but she was concerned that he had a copy of the other waveforms. He really did have spies at Belfore.

"Draw what you heard, or you're going back into the Void."

"Where's my glass of water and something for my headache?" she asked. "At the moment, the only thing I can hear is the pounding in my head."

The Prophet gestured to a woman standing behind him, and she fetched a cup of water.

Andi took the cup in one hand and the marker in the other. She slowly sipped the water, trying to decide what she was going to do. Her dry mouth soaked up the liquid like a sponge, and it made her feel better. She believed she could render something that would represent what she heard in the Void, but she didn't want to hand over that information right off the bat. She didn't want to die either. If it came down to it, she would give him whatever he wanted. But she needed to hold something back, or there would be nothing to negotiate with.

She approached a whiteboard and wasted as much time as she could drawing axes and tick marks. She erased them several times and started over. When it became obvious that she was stalling, the Prophet struck the whiteboard with both hands hard enough to knock it over. There was a loud crash, and one of its wheels spun around for several seconds.

"Shall we proceed, Miss Fyffe?"

Andi went to the next whiteboard and scribbled a line that represented one of the resonator channels. She didn't try too hard to get it exactly right, but she provided enough detail to make it look legit.

One of the researchers pressed a button on his console and transferred an image of the drawing to the nearest workstation. He entered a sequence of commands to digitized the waveform and set the computer to work on the data.

Andi cleared her throat. "Headache," she said and pointed to her temple. "Can I get something for it, now? And while you're at it, how about some vegan cheese and crackers? I'm starving."

The Prophet ignored her requests as he waited for the preliminary analysis of the data. A minute later, the man at the workstation looked back at him and nodded.

"It looks as though your abilities are not just a myth." The Prophet smiled.

Andi feared she gave away too much information, and they might not need her around anymore.

"Comprehensive analysis of the waveform will take some time." He looked at the guard hovering a few feet behind Andi. "Store her in the barracks until we need her again."

Andi looked around the chapel at the cult members. Many of them had their hoods up, but the faces she could see radiated excitement. She struggled to believe that such a simple drawing could generate such a reaction. Then again, Bryan and Vance had a similar response when she solved the twin's puzzle.

CHAPTER 29

THE GREAT ESCAPE

A guard shoved Andi back in the barracks and slammed the door behind her. He punched in a code on a keypad, and the locking mechanism made a motorized whine as the bolts engaged. The sounds from the lock were like the touch-tones produced by an old telephone. Andi had been cracking them since the sixth grade when her best friend Trish wouldn't tell her the phone number of a boy she had a crush on. Trish called Johnny three times in front of her just to rub it in. But Andi played the sequence of tones in her mind over and over until she got home. She went straight to her dad's study and pressed every button on his phone until she figured out the number. By the next week, she had lost interest in Johnny, but thanks to Trish's selfish behavior, she had a way out of her confinement. She just needed to get rid of the guard.

"I never got anything for my headache," Andi shouted at the door and banged on it with her fist. Her head really did hurt, but it wouldn't stop her from getting out. "Hey, are you listening to me?" she shouted.

"Keep it down in there," the guard said.

"The Prophet said I would get something for my headache." She continued banging on the door even though it made the throbbing in her head grow worse. "I'm not going to stop until I get something."

She knelt on the floor and peered through the crack under the door. Feet shuffled back and forth and finally walked off. Her persistence was successful.

Andi jumped up and went to the keypad. She pressed all the buttons to learn the different sounds they produced, then she played back the sequence she had recorded in her mind until she matched each tone with a button.

Her plan was to open the door and exit the facility as quickly as possible, but she didn't know how to get out. The chapel was to the right, so her only choice was left. She looked at her robe and smiled. If they had left her in the frilly red dress, she would have stuck out like a sore thumb. She pulled her hood up and entered the five-digit code. The bolts retracted, and she cracked the door to peek out. The hallway was clear, and she headed left.

Andi saw a Ruttie approaching her. He wore a white robe, hood up, and stared blankly at the floor. Her insides trembled, but she was an actor. She could play a member of this crazy cult just as easily as she could the half-monster Caliban in *The Tempest*. She calmed herself, mimicked the other person's expression, and walked right by. He didn't even acknowledge her. Two more passed her, but nobody noticed—or cared. She wondered if the Prophet had everyone trapped there. Maybe they didn't mind her roaming around because there wasn't a way out.

A siren started blaring over speakers in the ceiling, and Andi dropped her casual front and sprinted down the corridor. She wanted to get as far away from the chapel as she could. The sound of voices echoed in the distance, but she kept moving to stay ahead of her pursuers. She stopped and jiggled every doorknob she passed, but none were unlocked. She eventually reached a dead end and panicked. Her fight-or-flight instinct was about to make a one-eighty. She knocked her hood back and made as aggressive of a stance as she could muster. She was ready for anything except the door opening up behind her. A man dressed in black reached out and grabbed her. He clasped his hand over her mouth and dragged her back into the room.

Andi tried to scream, but she couldn't. She tried to bite the man's fingers, but his gloves were too thick for her to do any harm.

"Calm down, Miss Fyffe," the man whispered. He closed the door behind them with his foot but didn't let go of her.

Andi recognized his voice and stopped struggling. He let go of her, and she turned around.

"Special Agent Hayden!"

She wanted to hug him, but she didn't think they were out of danger yet. One of the cult's guards was unconscious on the floor. His hands were zip-tied behind his back, and tape covered his mouth.

"My team has been following you since you left campus."

"Then why didn't you stop these crazy people from kidnapping me?" she asked, trying to whisper. "I thought they were going to kill me."

"It took time to get into the compound without being detected." He showed her a small tablet displaying a mosaic of video feeds. "I hacked into their surveillance system and have been monitoring your situation. I was coming to retrieve you, but you got free on your own. Nice job, by the way. How did you get through that lock so easily?"

"Trade secret." Andi smiled. "How are we going to get out of here?"

"When the hallway is clear, we can backtrack down to the next junction. There's a way outside if you have a key." He held up a credit card-sized piece of plastic between his fingers like the ace of spades. "I got it off of him." He nodded toward the man on the floor.

The video feeds on the tablet showed two different teams of security guards searching the corridor on the other side of the door. One guard tried to turn the doorknob, but Hayden had locked it. When the tablet showed the corridor was clear, they proceeded to the exit. Hayden tried to use the key, but it didn't work. He threw the card on the floor and kicked the door down instead. More alarms sounded, but they were outside and moving away from the compound before anyone responded.

Surprised that it was night, Andi looked at her watch. The hands hadn't moved since the last time she had checked it. They were stuck at 8:35 and 22 seconds, and she guessed that was when they dropped her into the Void.

"It's a couple of klicks to the transport. Are you able to make it?"

"Yes," she said. "I just want to get away from here."

The lightweight sandals they put on her were not the most appropriate footwear for traipsing through the woods, but she wouldn't let them slow her down.

Half an hour later, they arrived at a black SUV where Agent McKenzie was sitting in the driver's seat talking on a cell phone. She handed it to Andi. "It's your father."

Andi took the phone. She heard her father before she even put it up to her ear. "Hello. I'm fine. I'm fine."

McKenzie took the phone back. "Dean Fyffe, we'll be back within the hour. I just wanted you to know she was safe."

Andi got in the back seat. Her mind raced. A crazy cult had kidnapped her. They dropped her into the Void, and the FBI rescued her in the nick of time. Her brain was also filled with the weird hum from inside the Void. She felt pretty lucky, but her head was still pounding.

"Do you have anything for a headache?"

CHAPTER 30

THE REVELATION

Andi stretched out on the sofa in the dormitory's common room. She propped her feet up on an armrest and covered her face with an instant cold pack. The FBI medic had clipped a pulse ox on her index finger. It beeped every few seconds, but he assured her that the throbbing in her headache was consistent with hypoxia and would go away if she rested. She wanted to take a nap, but she needed to prepare herself for the imminent lecture from her father.

The elevator dinged, and the bustle of agents quieted. She couldn't see anything through the cold pack, but her time had run out.

"What were you thinking?" Dean Fyffe asked. His tone was full of both scorn and disappointment.

Andi lifted the edge of the cold pack and glimpsed her father standing in front of Bryan and Vance. They had been on the elevator with him.

"And what were you two thinking? They could have killed her," the dean said. "I should expel all three of you."

"You've already kicked me out of the program, so expulsion doesn't work for me." She adjusted the cold pack back on her eyes and waved a hand at the impotence of his threat.

"Maybe not for you, but it does for these two."

Bryan and Vance didn't utter a word.

"It's not a threat for them either," Andi said for them. "You can't meet the grant requirements if you expel just one of them." She spoke the truth. Bryan and Vance were just too afraid to defend themselves.

"I don't care about the grant," her father said. His volume had increased along with his exasperation. "There are more important things in this world than risking your life to perform in some silly play."

Andi ripped the cold pack off her face and stared him in the eyes. "That's exactly what that crazy cult guy said." She raised herself, trying to minimize the pounding in her head. "Look, I didn't die. They just wanted information." She didn't tell him about her trip into the Void because she didn't want to kill him with a heart attack in a room full of FBI agents.

Special Agent Hayden walked over and interrupted. "Your father warned us you might not take our protection seriously."

Andi shook her head. "It's hard to imagine that anyone would kidnap me to further their Void research. I should be the last person on anyone's list."

"What did they want?" Hayden asked.

"They wanted me to draw some waveform patterns."

"Is that something from your research here at the university?"

She laughed. "I didn't do any research. I was a glorified tour guide."

"Then why did they want you?" he asked.

"The cult leader said his spies here at Belfore told him I solved this goofy puzzle for Bryan and Vance. He wanted me to solve another one."

"Wait a minute," Vance said. "Only Bryan and I knew about that... and the twins... and probably their parents... and maybe some of the techs... and I might have bragged about it to another grad student." He stopped after he realized what he had said.

Hayden's eyebrows raised. "Solving a puzzle got you abducted by a cult?"

"Nuts isn't it?" Andi said and made a sideways smile.

The radio clipped to Hayden's belt beeped, and he walked over to the other agents. The dean followed him, but Bryan and Vance sat on either side of Andi on the sofa. They both stared at her.

"What?" she said. "You two are creeping me out."

Bryan whispered, "What did they have you listen to?"

Andi whispered back, "You're not going to believe this, but they dropped me into the Void."

"Dude," Vance said. "Are you sure?"

Andi squinted one eye at him. "Yes, I'm sure. They made me wear a protective suit, stuffed me inside a coffin-like container, and dropped me through an open portal."

"And you survived," Vance said.

"Obviously," she said. "But this headache is killing me." She rubbed her temple, hoping to massage away the pain.

"What did you hear inside the Void?" Bryan asked.

"There were two of those harmonic resonators you talked about. They were built into that weird suit. I had to tune them with several knobs to get a hum like the one from the puzzle."

"And?" Bryan said.

"And, you know, I did my thing." She grinned.

"What did you bring back?" Vance asked.

"I got some new waveforms, but I couldn't tell you if they were worth risking my life for."

"What did the cult do with the information?" Bryan asked.

"Well, I didn't give them the whole set, but they were pretty stoked about what I drew for them."

Vance stood, unable to contain his excitement. The FBI agents turned to look at his abrupt action, and he casually sat back down. "We need to get this data to the twins."

"How are we going to do that?" Andi asked.

Vance pulled out a tablet from his backpack and set it on the coffee table. He flipped through several screens until he found a drawing app and handed Andi a stylus. "Draw the waveform, and I'll send it to them."

Andi drew a figure. "This is what I gave them. It's correct but crude."

"Wow," Bryan said.

"Wow is right," Vance said.

Andi flipped her hand at them. "That's nothing." She drew six more graphs with considerably more detail. "I'm not sure, but these two felt like they were on a horizontal plane, and these two were on a vertical plane. I could tell by the way I moved my head."

She wrote an "H" and a "V" on the corresponding drawings.

Bryan and Vance both looked like they had just won the lottery.

"Does this mean anything to you?" she asked.

"You've probably jumped Voidology ahead by thirty years," Vance said. "We'll have to wait and see what the twins say, but wow. I mean, WOW."

"You already said that," she said.

Vance jotted some notes on the drawing and sent it as an encrypted email.

Bryan took the tablet and looked at the drawings. "I knew you could do it."

"What was it like in the Void?" Vance asked.

"Cold, dark, and weightless," she said, "but it was surreal."

"Were you in for the full aperture?"

"I think so. I sort of passed out at the end."

"How far were you inside?"

"The portal looked like it was several hundred feet away. It was just a bright star in the darkness."

"The Void is likely a nonlinear dimension. One foot is a hundred feet or something like that," Vance said.

"Also, that cult has a bigger induction coil than Belfore, and there were at least a hundred researchers there, maybe more."

"No way," Vance said. "How could they make a bigger coil? Belfore's is the largest one ever fabricated."

"I'm just telling you what I saw."

"Are you sure?"

Andi narrowed her eyes again at Vance.

"Okay." He raised his hands in surrender.

Andi picked up the TV remote on the coffee table and surfed through the channels until she found a twenty-four-hour news network. "I thought I might have been breaking news." She sounded disappointed.

"I don't think they've told anyone," Vance said. "Not until they figure out what's going on."

"Look, there's Brit Devereaux," Andi pointed at the newscaster on the TV. "She's one of Belfore's most famous alumni."

"I've seen her before," Bryan said, "but I didn't know she went to school here."

"That reminds me of something," Andi said. "I have a pretty good idea who the cult leader is." Andi turned to Bryan, who was still looking at the tablet. "Can you bring up the video of the first portal opening?"

Bryan did a quick search on the internet and found the video. The footage shot by the news crew had captured the event in all of its gruesome details.

"Oh, yeah," Bryan said. "She's the interviewer in the discovery video."

"Not that video," Andi said. "The unedited one."

Bryan did another search and played the original footage.

"There," she said and pointed at one of the men in the video. "That's him. He doesn't look exactly the same, but his voice is unmistakable."

"That video is thirty years old. How can you tell it's the same guy?" Vance asked.

Andi pointed to her ear.

"That's Jonathan Rutledge's lab assistant," Vance said. "Daniel Moody, I think."

"Listen to the guy asking the interview questions. You never see his face, but he was there too."

"Didn't Daniel Moody claim the induction coil was his idea and Jonathan Rutledge stole it from him?" Bryan asked.

"That's right," Vance said. "He got booted out of the university for making that claim. Nobody would publish his papers, and he ended up traveling around giving lectures on the Void."

"What if he really did come up with the idea for the induction coil?" Andi said. "It's possible. We're all familiar with how Rutledge's son turned out. Maybe the apple didn't fall far from the tree."

Vance shrugged.

"How do you go from an uncredited assistant to a cult leader?" Andi asked.

"And how is their research so much more advanced than Belfore's?" Vance asked.

"And why is a cult secretly researching the Void in the first place?" Andi asked.

CHAPTER 31

THE STAGED

PRODUCTION

"It's so easy to manipulate a stupid little girl," the Prophet said from his throne in the sanctuary. "We wasted our resources staging such an elaborate Hollywood escape."

"We have a lot riding on this gambit," the suited man said. "Are you sure she bought it?"

"Hook, line, and sinker." The Prophet's smugness was well-practiced. He excelled as a puppet master, and he would never have grown his cult of followers so large otherwise.

"I feared she might think the tone-encoded lock was a little convenient," the suited man said.

"She's too simpleminded to realize we engineered her predicament. She wanted to be an actress. We're dealing with an individual who craves for someone to tell her what to do," the Prophet said.

"And Hayden?"

"A white knight riding in to save the day. It was serendipitous that the dean had asked him to keep an eye on the brat."

"It's a big risk letting her go back to Belfore," the suited man said. "She knows too much about our operation, and it's my responsibility to keep this facility off everyone's radar."

"She knows we're close by, but Hayden wound her through the dark countryside so much that she'll never be able to find her way back."

"You're lucky the FBI assigned Hayden to this case."

"Luck had nothing to do with it. He volunteered, saying he's an alumnus and familiar with the area. Besides, I had him bring the Interpol report of our covert activities to his supervisor's attention."

"Is the information she brought back from the Void worth all the effort we've put into this charade?"

"Absolutely," the Prophet said without hesitation. "I've never been so pleasantly surprised. Who would have believed this girl, with all of her ineptitude, held the key to unlocking the Void? It's unfathomable, but it's true."

"She will tell everyone what she saw, and that will cause problems for the Church."

"Hayden will moderate anything she says. Besides, we didn't get a full account of the information she acquired, and if we let that data make its way to those twins, we'll double the return on our investment."

"What if Belfore releases their findings before we do?"

The Prophet's face turned grim. "Are you familiar with the term *doomsday cult*?"

The suited man frowned.

"Don't worry," the Prophet said. "If it comes to that, we'll be on the other side of the country."

CHAPTER 32

THE TEAM

It was the first night Andi had spent in a dormitory. She learned that the tiny bed was rock hard, noise blared all night, and an unidentifiable aroma permeated everything. It disgusted her, but she fell asleep as soon as her head hit the pillow. She dreamed about being in the Void, floating through the undulating waves of distortion. The hum of the harmonic resonators repeated over and over. The sound haunted her subconscious mind, but it somehow soothed her too.

She woke up early the next morning and used the communal shower, another first, and realized that she didn't like the concept. There wasn't anyone else showering, but she could imagine it full of other naked people. After washing off the layer of cult residue, she dressed and banged on her neighbors' doors.

Bryan immediately came to his door, but she continued to pound on Vance's.

"It's 6:00 a.m.," Vance said after he cracked his door.

"I'm up," Andi said, "so you need to be too." She couldn't even see his face buried in his poofy, bed-head hair.

While she waited for Bryan and Vance to get dressed, she scanned the spread of donuts the FBI had set up in the common room. She was starving but doubted any of the fried rings were remotely vegan. She filled a cup from a single-serve coffee maker and made do.

Bryan joined her but didn't get anything for breakfast.

Vance followed with four donuts stacked in his palm. He had a tablet in his free hand and repeatedly blinked as he tried to focus on the screen. When he read the waiting message, a grin formed on his face.

"What's up with you?" Andi asked as she cuddled the warm cup in her hands.

"We got an email back from the twins," he said. "They stayed up all night working with the new data."

Bryan yawned. "What do they think?"

Andi was also curious about what they might have discovered. She twirled her finger in the air to get Vance going again.

"The good news is that everything Andi retrieved from the Void was exactly what they wanted. They said it contained keys within keys."

Andi snorted. "Whatever that means." Then she frowned. "And what's the bad news?"

"They need more data to complete their equations."

Andi stood. "What?" The FBI agents looked at her, and she sat back down and spoke more softly. "I'm not going back in there again. Especially since I would have to go knock on insanity's door and ask if I can borrow some of their equipment and use their induction coil."

"I still think the test pod from my propulsion test would work," Vance said.

"But how do we protect Andi from the radiation?" Bryan asked.

"Thanks, Bryan. At least someone is looking out for me." Andi crossed her arms. "If the cult had a suit that protected me, why didn't they just stick a recorder inside one and drop that in the Void?"

"High magnetic flux wreaks havoc on circuitry, and the shielding must not protect electronics," Vance said.

"I don't seem to be any worse for wear," she said.

"Biology is pretty resilient when it comes to magnetic radiation," Vance said.

Andi frowned and looked at her wrist. "My watch stopped working after they put me in the Void, and it was in the suit."

"If the simple electronics used to vibrate a quartz crystal can't survive with shielding, the delicate equipment needed to record a resonator's output won't either."

"I wasn't the first person they've stuck in the Void either. The straps used to adjust the suit's fit were worn, and the fact that it was adjustable means it wasn't only for me."

Vance rubbed his short red beard. "The suit must have superconducting fibers to deflect the radiation, but it is hard to shield against magnetic fields. It would also need a power source capable of working in the Void. I don't know how they got that all to work."

"My flesh and DNA are still intact." She smiled. "My head doesn't even hurt today."

"We have nothing like that," Vance said. "How did they get such advanced tech?"

"Their goals differ from ours," Bryan said. "We're trying to solve a thousand pieces of the puzzle and create the building blocks to base our research on. They don't have to justify any of their experiments or share any of their results, and they can focus all of their efforts on a specific area of their choosing."

"They also don't have any ethics or concern for safety," Andi said. "How many poor souls did they stick in the Void before they got the suit working?"

"Probably a lot," Bryan said.

"They would have had to submerge people in the Void to see if it worked," Vance said.

"I told you they were crazy," Andi said.

"Maybe they used animals," Vance said. "We don't know."

"I bet they used their own members," Bryan said. "It's a cult after all."

"Why didn't you bring back one of those suits, Andi?" Vance asked.

"Hey, I brought back a lovely white robe. I'm sure it makes quite a statement in the cult world."

"What did the protective suit look like?"

"The outer surface was a wire mesh," Andi said. "It was dark gray, like the induction coil, but it was flexible."

"Can you be more specific about the mesh pattern?" Vance asked. "It might be possible to produce something like it with the fabricator."

She pursed her lips. "The weave looked similar to a sweater I once had."

"Can you draw the pattern like you did with the waveform?"

Andi sighed and shook her head. "I didn't hear the pattern of the wires."

"It was worth a shot." Vance smiled.

"Oh," Andi said, remembering something. "There was a box attached to the suit with a cable. It was wrapped in the same wire."

Vance rubbed his chin again. "The power supply? How did they come up with one that functions in the Void?"

"It was heavy," Andi said. "And about the size of a lunch box."

"Were there any controls or indicators?"

"No, it was just a box."

"How did they send you through the portal?"

"They locked me in a transparent, tube-like container and lowered it down through a horizontally mounted induction coil."

Vance nodded. "That's a great idea. We have so many limitations on our payload insertions. Dropping it down from above would solve a lot of them."

"You may be right, but their production was all about the drama," she said. "Probably a cult thing. It was in a big auditorium-sized room with the ring in the center. There was even a platform on top of the test chamber for that nut-job leader."

Special Agent Hayden approached them. "We'll escort you three to the lab."

"Great," Andi said sarcastically. "You do realize that I'm not part of the Voidology program anymore?"

"Would you rather stay here?" he asked.

"Andi, you need to come with us," Vance said.

Bryan nodded in agreement.

She couldn't believe she wanted to spend all day in the control room. Then she thought that might be a sign of post-traumatic stress disorder. "Oh, all right, let's go."

Vance and Bryan were excited to get back to their research. The gigantic influx of never-before-seen data that Andi provided had them so preoccupied they hadn't even thought about the cult or the FBI babysitting them. Andi, on the other hand, was bored out of her mind. She looked at her watch, but it still showed 8:35 and 22 seconds. She tapped on the face, but it wasn't going to work again. The monotony was making her reconsider her decision to be part of the team.

Special Agent Hayden returned Andi's phone and Bryan's bus pass. The FBI had recovered them from the theater when they processed the crime scene. But every time she picked up her phone, Hayden rushed over and told her not to use it, or she would give away their location. After his third warning, it surprised her that he didn't try to take it back, but she wouldn't have surrendered it. Bryan and Vance were so engrossed in analyzing the new data that she had to engage in other forms of entertainment, and conversation with Hayden was the only alternative.

"Has the FBI raided the cult's compound yet?" Andi asked him.

"It takes time," he said. "We have to get warrants and enough manpower to the rally point before we make a move."

"Where's the other agent? McKenzie? I haven't seen her since we've been back."

"She's providing intel to the task force. Nobody knows more about this cult than she does."

"Have you identified any of the cult's informants? Like the one who ratted me out?"

"Not yet," he said, "but nobody gets in here unless we've vetted them."

"What about the twins? They're in more danger than I am."

"We're fully capable of protecting the kids," Hayden said, but his tone showed he was growing tired of the questions.

"The cult knew about them and how capable they are. You probably need to increase their protection."

"We're on top of it, Miss Fyffe."

"Then what's next? Are we going to sit here forever?"

"We thought you would want to do your research like you would normally do."

Andi laughed. "You don't know me very well." She cocked her head toward Bryan and Vance. "Those two do appear oblivious to their captivity." She pulled out her phone again. "Can I make a phone call?"

"To whom?" he asked.

"I want to call one of my fellow players and see what happened at the performance I missed. You know, the one where I was about to make my acting debut, but a cult kidnapped me right before the curtain went up?"

Hayden mulled over her request. "Put the call on speaker and don't mention the investigation, your abduction, or your current location."

Andi dialed Alisha's number.

There was a click when the call connected. "What?"

"Hi, Alisha. This is Andi."

"Who?"

"Andalusia. Your understudy."

"Yeah? You're in deep trouble."

"Really?"

"An ambulance had to take David to the emergency room after you ditched him."

"Is he okay?" Andi asked, trying to show some concern.

"Nervous breakdown, they think."

"I didn't dit—" Andi started, but Hayden raised his hand and stopped her.

"I told him you weren't ready."

"But—"

"You shouldn't come to the theater anymore. It would just send David over the edge again. Okay? Gotta go."

The call ended.

Andi sighed. "That went pretty much how I expected. That cult cost me my one chance to get back in with the Dark Crowd Players. I'll never get another chance now."

"Perhaps that's a sign you should devote yourself to something more practical," he said. "Like these two gentlemen." He pointed at Bryan and Vance.

"I tried that," she said and crossed her arms. "I was getting comfortable with the whole idea, but my own father kicked me out of the program because he found another student to fill his precious grant slot."

"He might reconsider."

"Nope," Andi said. "It would cost Vance the financial support my father promised." She hadn't meant to say that out loud.

"What!" Vance swiveled his chair around. "I don't get any financial support."

"I asked my father why you had to work two dumb jobs and didn't get any support from the grant. He said he would look into it, and then he said I couldn't rejoin the program without jeopardizing your funding."

"Dude, you shouldn't worry about me," he said. "I appreciate you trying to help, but you belong here in the program just as much as I do."

Andi stared at Vance. "Are you feeling okay?"

"You've contributed as much or more to this program than anyone else," he said. "Don't you agree, Bryan?"

"You've contributed more than I have."

She shook her head. "I've only been able to contribute because of extraordinary circumstances, and I don't get kidnapped by a cult on a regular basis."

"I think you underestimate your ability," Vance said. "Look how fast you caught up on your classes, and besides, you're part of the team now."

"Are you sure you're feeling okay?" she asked again.

"He's right, Andi," Bryan said. "You're part of the team."

Andi blushed. She didn't know what to say.

CHAPTER 33

THE CONFIRMATION

The Prophet beamed atop his dais in the sanctuary. "Our in-depth analysis of the girl's waveform data is extraordinary. I haven't been this enthusiastic about my research in years."

"I suppose you were right about her holding back information," the suited man said.

"The data she provided us was a paltry ten percent of what she gave her colleagues."

The suited man frowned. "I've consulted with Hayden. He can only sustain the situation at the university for another day or two."

"Proceed with the doomsday plan to eliminate Belfore, but we must reacquire the girl before the final phase goes into effect. She's far too valuable to squander her talent."

"I guess she is a real human tape recorder."

"She's far more than that. If we could successfully put a tape recorder in the Void, it would capture only a fraction of the information she brought back."

"What more can she provide?"

"I've spent the last day studying the waveforms. As fantastic as they are, I don't have all the pieces needed to complete my model of the Void. There are still too many missing variables, and we must send her in again with a reconfigured resonator."

The suited man shook his head. "She won't cooperate."

"I've devised a plan for that." The Prophet grinned.

The suited man nodded. "It's risky to keep her involved with our enterprise."

"Extract the girl and make sure nothing happens to her."

CHAPTER 34

THE MISSING PIECE

The FBI shuttled Andi, Bryan, and Vance to the physics building each morning at nine. They remained in the induction coil's control room until five-thirty and were returned to the dormitory. After Andi's abduction, an agent guarded the maintenance shaft entrance at the end of the hallway. She didn't know if they worried about her leaving again—which she wasn't—or a cult member getting onto the floor.

Sequestration wasn't as bad as Andi had imagined. The FBI didn't want to eat from the cafeteria on the first floor either, and better food was brought in. The three students also had plenty of time to bond and ponder the world-changing discoveries. Andi recognized how incredible an experience the time was and enjoyed her new comradery, but there was a downside to protective custody. If she wanted something from her apartment, Hayden dispatched an agent to get it. She didn't like some strange man rummaging through her underwear drawer, but she didn't have a choice. She would have been much more comfortable with Agent McKenzie, the only female agent, performing this task, but she hadn't been seen since the rescue at the cult's compound.

When the trio arrived at the physics building on the fourth morning, a caravan of black SUVs filled the unloading zone. It was an odd change to their rigid routine, and Andi didn't find out what was up until she reached the control room. Four burly FBI agents were standing next to two little kids. It was an extreme contradiction of proportions. The twins smiled when they saw Andi.

Vernon ran over and grabbed her hand. "We need to talk to you."

Andi smiled. "Sure."

"We need more information on the waveforms."

Helena approached Andi. "Can you show us a different axial view of the data?"

Andi pressed her lips together. "I don't know. I just kind of drew what I thought they would look like."

The twins looked back at Vance and Bryan.

"If you give her an example of what you want," Vance said, "I bet she can figure it out."

Vernon grabbed a marker. He could only reach a foot above the bottom of the whiteboard, but he drew a 3D approximation of a waveform with an oblique perspective. "If you can produce something like this from the data you gathered, we can infer the missing variables."

Andi's eyes lit up. "And that means I would never have to retrieve more data?"

Both of the twins nodded vigorously.

"I can try," Andi said, "but I'm not sure I understand exactly what you want."

"I'll give you some examples to go by," Bryan said. He picked up a marker and drew a series of graphs. The first one was like the ones Andi had drawn before, but he incrementally oriented each subsequent graph until the last one resembled Vernon's.

Andi studied the drawings, but there was a big difference in looking at what the new graph should look like and getting her brain to make it happen.

Vernon had a tablet showing Andi's original sketches of the waveforms. Two of them had circles drawn around them. "Can you combine these into a new graph?" he asked as he handed Andi the device.

"No guarantees." She felt a little out of her element, and an audience now watched everything she did. She closed her eyes and searched for the information in her memory until she located the two graphs of interest. After trying a variety of operations in her head, she stopped. "I'm not sure I can do this."

"Sure, you can," Vance said, holding still in expectation.

Having the guy who once called her an incompetent tour guide now rooting for her was confidence building. She closed her eyes again and relaxed her mind, hoping it would instinctively know what to do. Combining different streams of audio data in her head was not something she had ever done, but she saw how the sequence of graphs Bryan drew changed. It took a couple of minutes of concentration until she felt the data coalescing and organizing itself into a new representation. She thought she was about to get it when a radio beeped requesting a status report. Andi's eyes popped open, and she stared at the agent who caused the distraction.

Vance asked, "Can some of you go out in the hallway? We need her to focus with no distractions."

Four of the agents left the room, but Hayden and another remained.

Andi drew some test graphs on the whiteboard and looked at the twins to see their reactions. They didn't light up like she wanted. She erased her previous attempts and tried again. This time she heard squeals before finishing. When she looked back, the twins were both grinning ear to ear.

"Do you want me to keep going?"

The twins nodded in unison, and she drew two more graphs.

Vernon held up the tablet and said, "Can you combine the last one you drew with this one?" He circled another graph on the tablet.

"Why not?" she said, hoping to ride her momentum. It required her to concentrate even harder, but she had a sense for what the twins wanted. She felt the pressure of needing to get the right answer, and it made her try even harder. There was a satisfaction in helping solve a mystery of the Void, even if she didn't understand what she was doing.

"There," she said.

Helena held up her tablet and took a picture of the whiteboard. The two kids ran over and hugged Andi's legs and giggled. They waved goodbye and left, followed by the FBI agents in the hallway.

"I think you did it," Vance said.

"Can someone please explain what I just did?" Andi asked.

"We'll need to wait until the little dudes get back with us to know for certain, but they seemed pretty stoked." Vance took a picture of the graphs and then erased the whiteboard.

Andi looked stunned after seeing her work disappear.

"We can't just leave that sitting out in the open," Vance said.

Hayden's phone rang, and he stepped outside the control room to take it. When he returned, he had a grim look on his face. "We're taking you to another location. The Rutties are on the move."

"What does that mean?" Andi asked.

"We don't know, but we've established too clear of a pattern in their behavior for any of you to remain at Belfore.

"Good grief," Andi said.

CHAPTER 35

THE REACQUISITION

It was noon before the FBI agents had all of Belfore's potential targets rounded up and ready for relocation. Andi, Bryan, and Vance were in the back seat of one SUV. Rutledge and two other professors in another. The FBI didn't disclose their destination for security reasons, but Andi thought the road train of black SUVs made them more conspicuous than ever.

Hayden rode in the front passenger seat of Andi's SUV. Another SUV drove in front of them and two behind. They had been on the road for about thirty minutes when the radio chirped twice. Hayden keyed the transmitter in response but said nothing. The front two SUVs pulled ahead of the back two. A loud bang rumbled behind them.

Andi jerked her head around to see balls of flames instead of SUVs on the road behind them.

"Oh my God," she squealed, knowing there were no survivors in the other cars.

Bryan and Vance were too stunned to speak.

Hayden and the driver showed no reaction to the event.

"Don't we need to stop?" Andi asked.

"Protocol requires us to continue to our destination as long as we're able," Hayden said.

"But those people…"

"There's nothing we can do for them."

"We could stop and make sure we're not going to blow up," Andi said.

"That's not the protocol."

"Don't you need to call somebody and tell them what just happened?"

"When we get to the destination," Hayden said with no emotion.

"This isn't right." Andi looked at Vance and Bryan. "Do you think this is right?" She leaned closer to Hayden. "We need to turn around and go back. Call somebody. Get on your radio. Do something." Andi was yelling and didn't even realize it.

"Remain calm, Miss Fyffe. We'll soon be at our destination."

Andi was not calm. In fact, Hayden's calmness raised her anxiety level. She didn't know what was wrong with him until the SUV turned off the highway and made its way through a wooded area, emerging at a large solar farm with a complex of oddly shaped white buildings. Her eyes grew larger as the severity of her situation sank in. It was dark when she last saw the cult's compound, but she immediately recognized it.

"This is that crazy cult's compound," she told Bryan and Vance. "This is where they took me before." She turned back to Hayden. "Why are we here?"

Hayden jerked around and glared at Andi. "If you don't shut up, I will use my FBI-enhanced chloroform on you again."

Anger replaced Andi's fear, and her nostrils flared. "You're the one who made me miss my performance!"

"Yeah, but I'm also the one who *saved* you." He laughed.

"You're one of those Rutties," she said.

"No, but I work for the Prophet, and he's very interested in you."

She snorted. "He's not interested in me, just the information his lackeys can't come up with on their own."

The SUV stopped, and a team of men dressed in white uniforms surrounded their vehicle. Hayden got out and opened the back door. The guards escorted Andi, Bryan, and Vance to the sanctuary where the Prophet waited for them on his throne atop the dais.

"Welcome back, Miss Fyffe." His smile was so big his teeth were showing.

"If you're only interested in me, you need to take Bryan and Vance back to Belfore."

"Nobody will want to be near Belfore in the next few hours." He smirked. "There will soon be a terrible accident when their little induction coil overloads and destroys the campus, possibly the whole town."

"You're crazy," she said.

"No, Miss Fyffe. I'm the Prophet."

"I know who you really are," Andi said, hoping to shock the man. "You're just bent out of shape because you believe you were cheated out of credit for that dumb ring. And after thirty years, you still don't have squat to show for it. Even if you did somehow come up with it, you're a one-hit wonder."

The Prophet's face turned red. He stood and stomped down the steps from his throne. Andi thought he was going to hit her, but she wasn't done.

"You're Daniel Moody, Jonathan Rutledge's lab assistant."

The Prophet stopped his descent.

"I recognized you from the viral video. That fat guy in the suit was the interviewer in the discovery footage, a.k.a. Jason Reed. Special Agent Hayden is obviously the soundman." She ran her finger down her forehead, matching the location of his scar. "He didn't say anything in the video, so I wasn't sure at first." Andi paused and scanned the room. "There was one more guy, the cameraman. What happened to him? Did he not approve of your fake cult?"

"Alan Jones was a member of my congregation, but we didn't see eye to eye on how to run things."

"Let me guess, you dropped him in the Void?"

The Prophet smiled. "Yes, he took communion."

"Just say it," she said. "You murdered him."

The Prophet descended the remaining steps and swung back his hand to slap Andi's face, but Vance grabbed his arm before he made contact. Two guards wrestled Vance to the ground, pushing his face into the polished stone floor. He groaned from the pain.

The suited man, Jason Reed, approached. "We're not getting anywhere with this confrontation. We need to get the girl back in the Void and finish the research before we eliminate Belfore."

"What does that mean?" Andi asked.

The Prophet laughed. "I'm going to overload Belfore's induction coil and erase that miserable campus from the face of the Earth."

"And kill my father?" she asked and crossed her arms. "I'll never help you."

"You'll change your mind when I place one of your friends in the immersion capsule with you without a ceremonial cassock. If watching one of them dissolve in front of you isn't enough, we'll try it again with the other."

CHAPTER 36

THE SURVIVORS

Twenty-Nine Years Earlier

"To the survivors," Daniel Moody said and raised his beer for a toast. "May we all get the credit we are due." He had already drunk too much, but it was a special occasion, the first anniversary of the Void's discovery.

Jason Reed followed suit. "To the survivors. May WHNV suffer a major ratings slump and regret firing me and my crew."

"To the survivors," Michael Hayden said. "May you each find a new career like I have."

"To the survivors," Alan Jones said. "May employment find the rest of us."

All four clinked their glasses and took a drink.

Moody sat his half-empty glass back on the table and stared at Hayden. "Why be a cop? That's quite a change from an audio tech."

"He thinks he's a badass because of that scar on his face," Jones said. Everyone laughed.

"If I can't be pretty, I want power," Hayden said. Everyone laughed again. "Besides, I was just doing the TV gig while I waited to get into the police academy."

"Maybe when you finish, you can arrest the thieves who stole my research," Moody said.

"I might be able to give them a traffic ticket," Hayden said and took a drink. "I can't believe the university won't give you any credit for the discovery."

"They say I was only a student in the physics department and never worked on the battery project, but the induction coil was my design. I came up with it. I'm the one who found a use for the new superconductor filaments. Jenny couldn't do anything with her theoretical work until I fabricated the induction coil, and Rutledge never did a thing but order us around and take credit."

Hayden shook his head. "That's low to cut you out of the discovery."

"It's worse than that. They threw me out of the program because I kept pushing them for credit. Then they banned me from the campus for life. I shouldn't even be at this bar right now."

"Jeez, can't you get a lawyer?" Reed ran his hand through his thinning hair. "There has to be a way to get credit for your work."

"I've tried." Moody sighed. "Before I ran out of money, my attorney said that Belfore owns all the research done at their facilities. Even if they acknowledged my involvement, I wouldn't have any legal claim on the work."

"That's crap," Reed said.

"What about you?" Moody asked. "Can't you sue the TV station for taking your segment?"

"The WHNV lawyers said the idea to do the battery piece was the station's, and we were all entry-level employees doing our jobs."

Moody laughed. "We all know that's not true. You set the whole thing up to get another chance with your ex-girlfriend, Jenny."

"Hey, she came to me. I didn't even want to do the segment, but I did it for Jenny." Reed had a somber expression.

"Belfore stole her work too," Moody said. "If she had survived, we could have fought the university together. It's only my word against theirs now."

"I would help you if I could, but I've got my own troubles," Reed said.

"I can see the TV station scamming you out of your credit, but why did they fire all of you?"

"Our termination letters said we were responsible for the equipment. Since we weren't able to pay for a $20,000 camera…" Reed dragged his finger across his throat.

"But your footage is the most-watched video in history," Moody said.

"And WHNV used it to make a national celebrity out of its roving reporter."

"The jokes on them," Jones said. "Brit Devereaux dropped them like a hot potato on her rise to stardom."

Moody narrowed his eyes. "I still don't understand how she got credit for your piece. She wasn't even there."

"They spliced her into the video to ask Rutledge the questions," Reed said. "Brit got so much publicity from it, she's now a regular on the Today Show. Nobody saw the raw footage for several months."

"That sucks," Moody said. "She had nothing to do with it, and she's the only one who got famous."

"Well, they just stole my career-making piece and fired me," Reed said. "Belfore stole your life's work and blacklisted you. I think you're the bigger loser." He made an "L" with his thumb and finger and held it up to his forehead.

"I'll get even one day. Mark my words." Moody stared into space for a second.

"Don't do anything crazy. I would hate to arrest you after you saved my life, but I will." Hayden smiled and drank the last of his beer.

"I do have some good news," Moody said. "I found a way to make some money."

"Really?" Reed's eyes widened.

"I've been traveling to universities in the area giving lectures on the Void. That's what they're calling it now."

Hayden snorted. "What a stupid name. Is that the best anyone could come up with?"

"Well," Moody said, "it's actually pretty accurate. I didn't like it at first, but it grew on me."

"If Belfore doesn't want you around, why do the other schools want you to give lectures?"

"Belfore's stingy with the information they have on building an induction coil, and everyone wants a piece of what they think will be the biggest discovery of the century."

"If you can't get any credit for the discovery, why would anybody listen to you?" Reed asked.

"Nobody knows more about fabricating the coils than I do." Moody smiled. "It was my idea."

"Won't Belfore sue you?" Reed asked.

"They can try, but my attorney said they can't stop me without proving I didn't come up with the design. But they can't claim my work on the induction coil is their property while simultaneously saying I never worked on it at all. They have to pick one, and they decided to ignore me completely."

Reed furrowed his eyebrows. "How much do you get for a lecture?"

"I started out asking $500, but I'm up to $2,000 now. My plan is to keep raising the speaker fee until someone balks."

"Wow. How many lectures do you have scheduled?"

"Ten. I just haven't had time to round up anymore."

There was a gleam in Reed's eyes. "What if I help you out? Like a manager?"

"Hey," Jones said. "I can be your assistant manager."

"I could use some help," Moody said. "But the Void may be a fad, and people might lose interest."

"Something is better than nothing," Reed said.

Alan nodded.

Moody looked at Hayden. "You want in too?"

"I'll pass, but thanks for the offer. If law enforcement doesn't pan out, I reserve the right to change my mind."

"How many people attend these lectures?" Reed asked.

"About a hundred, but it's been increasing," Moody said. "A few people show up at every one. It's strange."

"Like groupies?" Hayden asked.

"I guess," Moody said. "They're crazy weird. All they want to know is how they can use the Void to find God."

CHAPTER 37

THE REDUX

The guards shepherded Andi and Vance through the maze-like corridors of the Church until they reached an elevator.

"Where's Bryan?" Andi asked. Her commanding tone didn't reflect the defenselessness of her standing. "Why isn't he with us?"

There was no reply to her questions, only scowling faces.

The elevator dinged, and the group rode up several floors to the staging area above the communion hall.

A robed attendant waited with a single protective suit. She was the woman who helped Andi get into the suit before, but her younger assistant wasn't there. The Prophet's threat was still fresh on her mind, and she hoped Vance wouldn't be sent with her into the Void. She would do whatever they wanted as long as they didn't harm her team, but she wouldn't surrender more information than necessary.

She sat on a bench and started to pull off her shirt when she noticed that three guards and Vance were staring. "Hey, creepos." She twirled her finger in the air. "Turn around." Vance complied immediately, but the guards waited until the robed woman nodded.

Andi stripped down to her underwear and slipped into the suit. She didn't have the claustrophobic feeling she had the first time, but the attendant hadn't attached the faceplate either.

When the guards and Vance turned back around, Andi was fully suited except for an oval-shaped opening around her face. The attendant attached a rectangular box to her waist and plugged it into the suit.

"Wow," Vance said and cautiously moved to inspect the protective suit.

"See, I told you. The wire mesh looks just like a sweater," Andi said.

"Do you know how this works?" Vance asked the woman.

He got a blank stare in return.

Vance pointed at the box. "What's inside there?"

To his surprise, the woman slid back several latches, allowing the box's front panel to swing open. Inside was a miniature induction coil nestled between rubber nubs. It was about the same size and shape as an actual donut. A bundle of wires ran from the bottom of the ring and coalesced into a heavy gauge cable that snaked its way through a port in the box's side.

Vance was wide-eyed. "That's a miniature induction coil. I've always been taught that the minimum diameter required to open a portal was around a foot. Can it open a portal? Is this the smallest one you have? What is it used for? I have a million questions."

Andi sighed. "They're using it to power the suit."

The woman nodded but said nothing as she resealed the box and made sure it was securely attached to Andi's waist.

"How did you know it's a power source?" he asked Andi.

"Jonathan Rutledge, or Moody, didn't plan to create a portal to the Void. That was an accident. They were trying to make electric car batteries." She looked at the silent woman. "Right?"

"I completely forgot about that," Vance said. "Forest for the trees."

The woman took Andi's hand and rested it on a new set of knobs sticking out of her suit's hood. Instead of three knobs of decreasing size on each side, it had four equal-sized knobs on just one side.

"I don't suppose I get some instructions on using these?" Andi asked.

The woman shook her head.

Vance looked at the knobs. "It looks like a modified reso-nator. I bet the first one had a fixed reception plane, that's why you got horizontal and vertical feeds. Three knobs prob-ably control an axis—X, Y, and Z. The last one might control the length of the superconductor filament, which vibrates in response to the electromagnetic radiation in the Void."

"That's super interesting," Andi said and shook her head. "But it doesn't tell me how to use it."

"You got the other resonators to work. Do what you did before," Vance said and rocked back and forth. "You seem awfully calm for someone who's about to take a plunge into the Void."

"Well," Andi said. "I survived the first time, and if they don't bring me back alive, I can't tell them anything."

"You've got a point, but I would need a change of underwear," he said.

Andi appreciated the support, but she worried that the robed woman was a little too forthcoming even if she didn't actually say anything. Vance being brought up to the staging area with her wasn't a good sign. He was likely going into the Void without a suit if she didn't cooperate.

"I don't understand how you do your... thing," Vance said and pointed to his ear. "But keep those orthogonal graphs the twins wanted in mind. That's what the little dudes wanted, so listen for whatever helps you draw that kind of graph."

Andi nodded.

"We may never be able to get them the data," he said, "but this may be our only opportunity to get it."

"You need to worry more about your own safety than solving the mysteries of the Void," Andi said.

"I know, but if you get another chunk of data, who knows what they'll be able to do. They might change the world." He smiled. "And you would definitely get to share the Nobel Prize with them."

The woman sealed Andi's suit with the transparent faceplate before she could respond to Vance. She had never paid attention to how truly committed Vance was to his research. She guessed that the members of the cult were too, but the Prophet had manipulated and twisted their cause. At least Vance's desire to learn more about the Void was genuine.

There was a click when the attendant connected an air canister to the suit, then she motioned for Andi to get into the transparent tube. Andi knew better than to resist, so she stepped into the container and turned around to face Vance. The woman swung the front half of the capsule back into place and locked the latches. Andi didn't panic this time. She controlled her breathing and remained calm. She wanted to be prepared. Maybe she could use it to bargain for Bryan and Vance's safety, maybe even hers too.

The capsule jerked when the hatch beneath it opened, and the pole extending from the ceiling lowered Andi down into the communion hall. Daniel Moody was not waiting on the platform to greet her this trip, and there was no overly dramatic ceremony to send her off. The hatch on top of the chamber opened, and her capsule dropped inside. The seal engaged, the air hissed, and the portal opened with a flash.

Andi's transition into the Void was just as smooth as her first trip. She didn't worry about dying this time and prepared herself for zero-G. The lights grew dim, and the temperature dropped. She started adjusting the dials on the side of her head and listened for the hum. The knobs were different, but they still worked like the first ones. She tuned in the strongest signal with the first knob and progressively refined it with the others. It took her a few tries to get the sound profile she wanted, then she closed her eyes and went to work.

Andi imagined herself in the language lab sealed up in a booth. She couldn't have asked for a better environment to use her ability. She didn't suffer from motion sickness this time, and she thought the lack of gravity made it more comfortable and easier to concentrate. Floating in the middle of the cylinder, she cleared her mind and pulled in the information.

The capsule abruptly stopped when the insertion reached its apex. Andi's momentum did not stop, and she rebounded off the floor with her butt. The power source box came unhooked from her suit and ricocheted off the curved wall causing its front panel to spring open. A bright light beamed out of the box like a floodlight.

Andi held up the power supply to her face and squinted to filter out its brightness. What she saw was impossible. There was an opening in the box, and through it was a forest with trees reaching into a blue sky striped with wispy clouds. The view filled the entire box and was clear as being there. It made no sense to her. Where was the miniature induction coil? Did it create another portal? The glow of the forest was so inviting she couldn't resist reaching into the box. She hesitated at first, just dangling her fingers inside the opening, then she stuck her whole arm in. She felt a warmth through the suit, and her hand brushed against a tree limb. It was incredible.

The immersion capsule jolted again and started moving out of the Void. Tree branches whipped against Andi's hand and she jerked her arm out of the box. The view through the opening was moving by so quickly that it became a blur. She could only make out colors changing between shades of green and brown.

As Andi approached the portal in the communion hall, the view through the box faded. The immersion capsule grew dark. She tried to reach inside the box again, but this time she could only feel the miniature ring.

Andi closed up the front panel of the box and hung it back on her waist. Gravity would resume as soon as the capsule left the Void, so she maneuvered herself in the weightlessness to get her feet flat on the capsule's floor. She wished she had more time to figure out what to do with all the information she had gathered, but she didn't.

The pole attached to the immersion capsule lifted Andi up to the staging area above the communion hall. She hadn't been conscious at this point on her first trip, and she didn't know how the first trip ended.

The robed woman opened the capsule door and removed Andi's faceplate.

Vance stared at her like she was on fire. "Are you okay?"

"I'm fine. I think I'm getting used it." She smiled. "I think I need a new title, like Void-o-naut." She shook her head. "That sounds stupid."

Vance nodded.

Andi sat on the bench and picked up her clothes. She stared daggers at the guards until they turned around. Vance didn't get the hint until she twirled her finger in the air again.

"Did you hear anything new while you were in the Void?" he asked, facing the wall.

Andi desperately wanted to tell Vance what she had discovered, more than anything, but not in front of their captors. Even then, she wasn't sure he would believe her until she saw a single strand of green caught in the suit's mesh right above her wrist.

CHAPTER 38

THE TRAITOR

The guards escorted Andi from the staging area down to the main level. Vance didn't go with her. She felt her stress level rising the farther apart they got. She almost threw out some caustic insults at her captors, but it wouldn't do any good. What she really wanted to do was discuss her discovery in the Void with her team. Maybe they would have an idea for why a passageway to a forest suddenly appeared in the lunchbox? It didn't matter if she understood what happened or not because she knew it was the world's biggest secret. If she had to, she would use it to negotiate for their lives, and that gave her confidence that there might be a way out of her predicament.

Daniel Moody stood on a platform in the center of the chapel with his flock surrounding him. Andi thought it was weird how he always had to be elevated above everyone else. It must have been a cult thing. Everyone had to look up with respect, but she could cast her contempt at him from any level.

"I hope your communion was enlightening," Moody said in full prophet mode.

Andi didn't respond. She thought he looked like the cat who had just eaten the proverbial canary.

"It's time for you to share God's message."

The guards herded Andi to a whiteboard along the wall, and a young man in a robe rushed over and handed her a marker. He gawked at her like a star-struck fan.

"Share the wisdom, Miss Fyffe," Moody commanded.

Andi did nothing. Running down the corridor, screaming and hoping she would get away, wasn't an option. Her life wasn't the only one at stake anymore. She shook her wrist at Moody and yelled, "You ruined my watch."

"I'll get you a thousand watches if you bring us closer to God."

"This was my mother's watch, and you can't replace it."

Moody's face turned rigid. "You're stalling, Miss Fyffe."

"I don't know what you want me to do. It was a fluke I got something useful the first time."

"I'll clarify," he said stone-faced. "Give us the waveform information recorded in your head, or I will sacrifice one of your friends to the Void. Is that clear enough?"

"Why should I believe you won't do that anyway?" Andi could tell by his wrinkled expression that the Prophet wasn't accustomed to anyone questioning his orders. She didn't care. She had no problem with conflict, especially when it was with a bully like him.

"I'll give you one more chance, Miss Fyffe."

"Really, I don't know what you want me to do." She was stalling, as Moody said, but her response seemed reasonable. There wasn't an established protocol for using her special ability. He didn't have a clue how it worked. As far as that went, she didn't either. "Can you get me some vegan M&M's?" she asked. "They help me concentrate."

Moody clapped sarcastically. "I expected you would be less than forthcoming with the information, and I've already made arrangements to motivate you." He raised his hand and pointed toward the corridor.

A flurry of activity ensued as his robed entourage cleared out of the chapel. Two of them rolled a portable whiteboard down the corridor, and the guards ushered Andi behind them. When they reached the communion hall, Andi's mouth dropped open. The transparent container sat on top of the test chamber with Vance inside. He was clad only in his worn-out T-shirt and faded jeans, and the induction coil beneath him was projecting the Rutledge effect onto the round walls of the communion hall.

Moody gestured up at Vance. "Perhaps this will incentivize you, Miss Fyffe."

The whiteboard stood next to the chamber, giving Andi a clear view of Vance's situation. She could see the bottoms of his feet through the transparent material, centered in the outline of a hatch. The induction coil emanated vibrations as it neared the power threshold, and the portal rested on the verge of opening.

Andi just stared at the blank whiteboard. Her mind raced to come up with a different option.

"Draw!" Moody yelled.

She turned back and looked at him. "As soon as you get Vance down from there," she said, "I'll draw the waveform."

"If you don't provide me with the information, there will be no use for you either," Moody said. "And I'll offer both of you to the Void."

"I don't believe you." She knew it was a risk to taunt a crazy man, but she was going to test her boundaries. "You're too dependent on the information you think I possess." She smiled. "If you kill Vance, I'll never give you the information. If you kill me, you for sure won't get it."

Moody laughed. It was not the response Andi wanted.

"I've been waiting thirty years, Miss Fyffe. I can wait a little longer, and I doubt you're the only one with special abilities. Now I know what to look for." He raised his hand to give a signal. "Say goodbye to your fellow heretic."

"Stop," someone yelled from the crowd. One of the hooded members pushed his way through the others. "Andi, you have to help us."

"Bryan?" Andi's said. "Is that you?" Her voice quivered.

He pulled his hood back so she could see his face.

"What are you doing?" she asked with an uncertain tone.

"I'm part of the Church." Bryan stared down at the floor.

"What?" Andi's voice rose several decibels.

"I've always been a member." He wouldn't look at her.

"You're the spy at Belfore?" Her nostrils flared.

Bryan started to say something but nodded instead.

"I trusted you." Andi glared at the top of his head. She wished he would look up and see her fury. "You used me for this ridiculous sham of a cult. Oh my God!"

"I had to find out what's in the Void," he said.

"I don't care what's in the Void," she yelled at him. She didn't believe that was true anymore, but she said it anyway. "I thought you were my friend."

Bryan's head jerked up and looked her in the eyes. "I am your friend."

"You got me kicked out of the Dark Crowd Players, and you knew how much that meant to me." Andi's face flushed.

"That wasn't me," he said, shaking his head.

"That lunatic over there," she said, pointing at Moody. "He's using you and all these other morons to get revenge on Belfore and the long-dead Jonathan Rutledge. Your Prophet—she made air quotes—was a measly lab assistant who still thinks he didn't get enough credit for the accidental discovery of the Void."

There were gasps from the acolytes.

"Blasphemy," one of them said.

"The way to God is through the Void," Bryan said mechanically.

"What a cute little brainwashed cult-y thing to say."

"I only wanted to understand the Void. That's the truth."

"Good grief," she said. "This explains your weirdo clothes and goofy haircut. Oh, and your inability to act normal around other people." She crossed her arms. "I'm such an idiot. How did I miss it?"

"We're trying to find God, and you are the key."

"Spoken like a true Ruttie," Andi said. "By the way, your God isn't in there. I was just there, I know."

There were more gasps from the crowd.

"He will kill Vance if you don't help. All you have to do is draw the waveform, and they'll let him go."

Andi turned to face Moody and threw the marker at him. "Go figure it out yourself, you loser."

Bryan tried to grab Andi's hand, but she pulled away. "Andi, you've got to help. Just draw the graph," he pleaded.

"I don't believe for a second that Vance will be safe if I tell you anything. How many has your Prophet disposed of in this fashion? Has anyone ever disagreed with him or failed to live up to his expectation? What happened to them?" She bet Vance wasn't the first person to be in this position, and the silence from the crowd confirm her speculation

"It's time to speed this along, Miss Fyffe." Moody looked up at a camera. "Open the portal."

"Wait, wait, wait." Andi stepped over to the whiteboard and prepared to draw a graph. She wouldn't play with Vance's life. She had a dozen waveforms in her head this time, but Moody didn't know that. If she just drew one, it might buy her more time. She sketched a very detailed orthogonal graph like she had provided the twins. "There," she said. "Now, get him down."

Moody rubbed his chin as he studied the drawing. "There must be more than that." He turned around and glared at Andi.

"That's all." Andi raised her hands in mock surrender. "I combined several channels of information into one waveform. There's nothing else, I promise." She mimed crossing her heart with her finger.

"It's a shame we needed a freak-of-nature with an obnoxious mouth to pull the final secrets out of the Void. God must have sent you to test my congregation's resolve."

Andi smiled at the insult. "You're welcome," she said sarcastically. "Now, get Vance down."

"I applaud your extortion of Belfore, and for what, acting lessons?" Moody filled the room with a belly laugh. "How the mighty academic powerhouse has fallen. And they once again didn't know what was in their possession. I gave them the Void, and they banished me. You were the key to solving its mysteries, and they replaced you with the first student they found. We have a lot in common, Miss Fyffe."

"We're nothing alike." Andi shook her head. "I never wanted to be in the Voidology program. I did a favor for my father in exchange for what I wanted. My ability to remember the static patterns from inside the Void is just a coincidence. You know, like how your fancy battery opened up a portal to the Void?" She hesitated for a second. "I take back what I said. We are alike. We're both frauds."

Moody let her words hang in the air for a second. "I will reclaim the credit that Belfore stole from me, and I don't care what I have to do to achieve that goal."

"You're so wrapped up in revenge that you don't see what's going on around you. The Void doesn't belong to you, and it never will. You just want to make everyone else fail so you can win, and you have to cheat to do it. You're such a loser."

"In a fair world, you would be a celebrity. The little girl who wanted to be an actress but instead solved the biggest scientific mystery of all time." A frown formed on his face. "But you're in my world now." He laughed at her.

A chill went down Andi's spine. If she gave him what he wanted, he wouldn't let her or Vance go. It was false hope to think otherwise. She still had the secret about the exit window, but she wouldn't give him that. She would just be handing him the Void on a silver platter. At best, she might string the nightmare along for a little longer. She felt defeated, and she could see on Moody's face that he knew it.

Andi raised her marker to the whiteboard and started to draw another waveform. She had been so wrapped up in deciding what to do that she had ignored the itching in the back of her mind. The stress of the moment finally worked a question to the surface. If the twins didn't need additional information from the Void to complete their work, why did Moody? Were his people that less capable than the twins? What about Bryan? He had access to the same orthogonal waveforms she drew for the twins, so why did Moody send her back in the Void?

"From what I understand," Andi said, "this additional information isn't necessary to complete the equations. So, why are you so desperate to get it?" She turned to face Moody, still holding the marker up in the air.

Moody narrowed his eyes. "The data from your first communion is incomplete."

"Yeah, yeah. We all know that, Danny. I'm talking about the second series of graphs, like this one." She tapped on the whiteboard with the butt of the marker. "The twins didn't need any more information from the Void. They've most likely solved the equations by now and scooped you." Andi wobbled her head in victory.

Moody pushed through his followers and approached Bryan. "Is this true?" His tone was sharp as a knife.

Bryan didn't answer.

"Is it true?" Moody yelled.

Bryan nodded, and Moody slapped his face so hard, it knocked him down.

Moody stared at Bryan sprawled on the floor. "Explain your behavior."

"If you had the data, you wouldn't have brought Andi and Vance here, and they would have been killed at Belfore."

"These heretics are not your friends." Moody's tone dripped with disgust. "And I won't spare them because of my son's weak conviction."

Andi was knocked back by what she heard. She had to replay it in her mind to make sure she heard it correctly.

Moody turned to a guard. "Bring me his belongings and lock him in the interrogation room."

The henchman jerked Bryan off the floor, twisted his arm behind his back, and marched him off down the corridor.

Andi waved her hand in the air. "Wait a minute, are you saying Bryan is your son?" This wasn't the best time to be quizzing a deranged cult leader about his progeny, but she had to confirm.

"I have many children, Miss Fyffe. And I won't miss this one." Moody looked up at Vance. "And I won't miss that one either." He made a motion with his hand, and the induction coil flashed.

CHAPTER 39

THE INTERROGATION

ROOM

"I discovered something in the Void!" Andi blurted out her secret so quickly that she hoped Moody understood.

He flipped up a hand to pause Vance's execution. "This better be good, Miss Fyffe."

"I know how to get out of the Void from the inside. Get Vance down, and I'll tell you."

"You can't come up with anything more believable than that?" he asked and started to lower his hand.

"I have proof," she said and pulled the green fragment out her pocket. "Inside the Void, I reached through another portal, and this pine needle got stuck on the suit."

Moody took the green strand and examined it.

The suited man, Reed, approached. "She's conning you. She already had that on her."

Moody rolled the needle between his fingers with a jerky movement. "This needle is too flat to be a pine needle. It's from a fir, and there are no fir trees in this part of the country." He held it to his nose and inhaled. "It's also too fresh for her to have brought with her."

"Are you saying you believe her?" Reed asked.

"I'm not making it up," Andi said, eyeing him.

Moody smiled. "Then you have a lot of explaining to do, Miss Fyffe."

"As soon as Vance is safely down."

The room flashed when the 142-second time limit on the portal elapsed.

Moody had Andi taken to a holding room down the corridor from the communion hall. She didn't think a cult's compound could get any stranger, but she was wrong. The room's appearance was straight out of a police drama. The door had no knob, just a numeric keypad. A camera hung from the ceiling between two buzzing fluorescent lights. Another knobless door on the back wall went somewhere and was next to a large, built-in mirror. The room didn't have marble floors like the rest of the facility, just worn vinyl tiles. A table and four chairs made the room feel cramped. She wondered why a cult needed an interrogation room. Were the Prophet's followers not as loyal as she thought?

Andi didn't know where they took Vance, but she had watched the immersion capsule rise through the hole in the communion hall's domed ceiling. He may not be safe, but they weren't about to drop him into the Void either. She wasn't sure what to think about Bryan. Moody was so brutal to his own son that the anger toward her betrayer had been replaced with sorrow, but she would still give Bryan a piece of her mind if the opportunity arose.

Her broken watch still showed 10:15. She habitually checked it several more times over the next hour before she heard someone outside the room. She ran over to the door and closed her eyes. Hoping to record the key sequence in her mind when they entered the code, she was disappointed. There were no tones, only the sound of clicking keys and the buzz of a magnetic lock.

Two security guards entered, followed by Moody.

"It's time for details of your adventure in the Void," Moody said.

"Is Vance safe?" she asked.

"He is in the room next door, but his safety depends on your cooperation."

"And Bryan?"

"Are you truly concerned about the spy who reported all of your activities to me?" Moody smirked.

"Actually, I am." Andi stared at him, trying to figure out if he really had so little regard for his son or if it was part of his act. She couldn't tell.

"Don't concern yourself with him. I'll punish him appropriately for his crimes against the Church."

"What does that mean? A trip into the Void without a protective suit?"

"Perhaps." Moody pulled back one corner of his mouth and coldly stared at her.

"You're crazy," Andi said. There was no reason to keep her opinion to herself at this point.

Moody tilted his head and smiled. "Enlighten me on creating a portal inside the Void."

Andi knew he would need to verify anything she told him, and that might buy her some time. She hesitated for a second but told him the secret. "I used the miniature induction coil inside the lunchbox."

There was a tick of surprise on Moody's face. "We've used this type of battery pack in the Void hundreds of times, and they've never created a portal."

"They probably did," she said. "Did you ever open the box inside the Void?"

"Opening the box would expose the power source to the effects of the Void and render it inert, killing the immersion capsule's occupant."

"Obviously not," Andi said. "The box came unhooked and popped open."

"We've invested a great deal of research into the battery packs, and they simply do not work without the superconductor mesh shielding."

"So, you haven't opened the box in the Void?" Andi said with an air of superiority.

Moody didn't answer.

"The portal to the outside disappeared when I approached the exit." Andi saw that she hadn't convinced him, but she was telling the truth.

"You wouldn't be able to fit your arm through the center of a three-inch induction coil."

"That's the weird part," she said. "I couldn't even see the miniature coil after the exit opened. It filled the entire box, and I stuck my whole arm through it. That's how I got the pine needle."

"It's a fir needle," Moody said lost in thought.

"Whatever," Andi said.

"I need to verify your claim," Moody said and left with his guards.

CHAPTER 40

THE REUNION

Andi sat at the table in the interrogation room for at least two hours. It felt like hours, anyway. She didn't know for certain since her watch didn't work. She was hungry and thirsty, but nobody had been by to check on her since Moody left. The only thing she could do was plot her escape, but nothing practical came to her. When her patience ran out, she jumped out of her chair and headed to the door. She made a fist and was about to start pounding on the door when she heard a faint patter coming from behind her.

She whipped around but saw nothing. It was a pecking sound like someone tapping their fingernail on glass, and she followed it over to the mirror on the back wall. She cupped her hands around her eyes and tried to peer through the one-way mirror. It didn't block out all the light, but she thought something moved on the other side. She jumped when the door next to her clicked and opened a few inches. Then a hand reached out and grabbed her arm.

"Bryan," she said and exhaled. "You scared me half to death. What are you doing here?"

He put his finger to his lip and whispered, "I'm getting you and Vance out of here."

"Really? And how are you going to do that?" She sounded more annoyed than relieved by his declaration.

"I haven't figured that out yet."

"Where did you come from?"

"They locked me in another interrogation room. They're all connected by this hallway."

"And you got out?"

"They changed the codes on the locks, but they forgot to take my bus pass." He lifted the lanyard off his chest. "I jimmied the lock with it."

"There's a camera in my room. They know I'm not in there."

"The camera isn't real. They're just there to intimidate."

"Are you sure?"

"I've lived here my whole life, except for my time at Belfore. I understand how this place works better than anyone."

"Where's Vance?"

Bryan led Andi down the dim hallway past another window. They saw Vance sitting in a room just like the one Andi had been in.

"How many of these rooms do they have?" Andi asked.

"Five," Bryan said and tapped on the window to get Vance's attention and brought him into the hallway.

"Dudes," Vance said. He grabbed Andi and Vance and gave them a big hug. "I wasn't sure I would see you again."

"Keep your voices down," Bryan said. "We don't want to attract any attention."

"What's with the white robe?" Vance asked, looking at Bryan.

He just looked at the floor and didn't respond.

Vance turned to Andi.

Andi groaned. "You didn't hear any of what transpired?"

Vance shook his head. "I couldn't hear anything in that capsule, and I was sort of preoccupied with the open portal beneath me."

"Well, our so-called friend here is a Ruttie. He always has been. That robe is his normal attire. He was the spy at Belfore. Oh, and he's also the son of the Prophet, a.k.a. Daniel Moody, a.k.a. the mad scientist who's about to blow up Belfore."

Andi marched over to Bryan. She waited for him to look at her, but he wouldn't. She had her verbal assault queued up and ready to deploy, but she stopped and looked back at Vance. "Before I read him the riot act, is there anything you would like to say?"

Vance looked like a deer caught in headlights. "I'm... in shock," he said.

"You're not much help." She swung her gaze back to Bryan like a club. "And what do you have to say for yourself?"

Bryan continued to look down. "I didn't want anyone to get hurt. I was trying to keep you safe."

Andi took in a deep breath. "People were killed." Her volume was too loud, and she reined it in a little. "It's no secret that I didn't care for Rutledge. He was a worthless boob, but I didn't want him blown up. He had a wife and a daughter. And what about the rest of the people in those SUVs? They certainly didn't deserve that."

Bryan raised his head. "I knew nothing about that, and I was just as surprised as you were about Special Agent Hayden working for my father."

Vance finally found something to say. "You were stealing our research?"

Bryan looked at Vance. "It was the only way I could end this."

"End what?" Andi asked.

"The Church. This cult," he said. "If someone solved the mysteries of the Void, there would be no reason for this place to continue, and we would be free."

Andi snorted. "I hate to break this to you, but Moody's going to disappoint you on that."

"Dude, you stole our work and gave it to these people?" Vance asked.

Bryan's posture stiffened. "I took information from Belfore, but I gave information back too."

Vance crossed his arms. "Like what?"

"I told you I found those dissipation trials in the grant repository, but they came from the Church. I steered you away from the monomer catalysts in your propulsion materials. I knew they wouldn't work. I introduced the superconducting mesh in my research, so someone else might try it. All of that tech came from here."

"So, your portal tracking idea came from here too, and you passed it off as your own? That's not cool, man."

"No," Bryan said. "It was all my work except for the shielding."

Vance shook his head.

"I also volunteered to tutor Andi so the program would meet the grant requirements, and I told you about her ability. I had a feeling she was the key to pushing our research along, and I was right."

Andi ran her fingers through her hair. "But you shared my secret with this cuckoo cult?"

Bryan shook his head. "I didn't. I swear. There are probably a dozen people at Belfore working for my father. I don't know who they are. They were watching me too."

"There were techs in the control room when Andi averted our potential meltdown," Vance said. "They might have pieced it together." He glanced at Andi to see if she was buying his train of thought.

"That's not enough to convince me," she snapped.

"I bet they bugged the place," Vance said. "We've talked about what you can do several times in the control room."

Andi shook her head. "We talked about the orthogonal graphs with the twins in there too, but nobody here knew about them."

"It takes forty-eight hours for the information to get back to the Church," Bryan said. "There hasn't been time."

"Hayden saw me draw the graphs for the twins," Andi said.

"But he didn't understand what you did," Vance said. "He's not a scientist. He didn't get why the twins were so excited or how totally incredible your graphs were."

"Everyone at the Church believed Andi had to go back into the Void to retrieve more data," Bryan added. "There was no reason to think otherwise."

Andi's face twisted up as she reconciled everything she had just heard. Then something filled her with dread. "What exactly are they planning to do at Belfore?"

Bryan hesitated. "Overload the induction coil. The explosion will take out the whole campus."

"No way," Vance said. "Overloading the coil won't release that much energy. At most, it might take out the test chamber and the auditorium."

"The Church has made a lot of discoveries," Bryan said. "One of them involved linking two induction coils together and simultaneously energizing them. When the portals open, they tear a hole in the boundary between our reality and the Void. Everything around the breach gets sucked in."

"That's not possible," Vance said with complete confidence.

Bryan nodded. "Remember the earthquake last year? It only registered 3.5 on the Richter scale at Belfore, but it resulted from two interlocked rings. They overloaded a thousand feet underground in an abandoned water well."

Vance paced around in the hallway. "They would have to break into the physics building and attach another induction coil to Belfore's ring. That's not possible," Vance said, shaking his head.

"You already suspect a tech is involved," Bryan said. "They would have access to all the equipment, and nobody would give them a second look."

"But rings are fabricated as a single piece. You can't link another one with Belfore's."

"They've been making modular rings here for years," Bryan said. "They are cheaper and easier to produce. If a ring the size of Belfore's is overloaded with another ring, even a much smaller one, the results will be catastrophic."

Andi softened her posture. "A weapon of mass destruction that would take out the last Void research facility, and nobody would question it being anything but a terrible accident. There would be no evidence left behind to prove otherwise."

"This is insane," Vance said. "What have you people been doing here?"

"More importantly, how are we going to stop them?" Andi asked. "My father is in the physics building, not to mention the 20,000 students and faculty on campus."

"We've got to tell someone," Vance said.

"If you haven't noticed," Andi said, "a cult has us locked in a room."

"How did you escape before?"

"I listened when they unlocked the door, and I got the code. But when they opened the door earlier, there weren't any tones."

"None of the doors here have ever used tone encoded locks," Bryan said. "I'm sure that was for your benefit, so you would believe you were escaping on your own."

"I can figure out the lock code," Andi said. "It just won't be as easy as the other one."

"There have to be guards outside the doors, so it wouldn't matter if we could get one open or not," Vance said. "And they're watching everything on those cameras hanging from the ceiling."

"The cameras are fake," Andi said.

"How do you know that?"

Andi pointed to Bryan.

"What else do you know?" Vance asked.

"Is there a secret way out of here?" Andi asked.

Bryan shook his head. "This hallway only connects the backs of the interrogation rooms. The only way out is through one of the rooms."

"If we get out of here, where can we go?" Andi asked.

"The compound is like a prison. The main entrance is the only way to get in or out."

"But I got out before," Andi said, "and it wasn't through the front door."

"You had inside help," Bryan said. "They never believed you would give them all the data, and they orchestrated your escape so you would share it with me."

Andi's lips flattened. She was still processing his betrayal, and she knew he risked a lot trying to keep her and Vance from being blown up at Belfore. He was still helping them, but the wound was fresh. She didn't have time for that to be a distraction now.

"If we got some of those white robes," Vance said, "we can move around without being noticed."

"And we only need two," Andi said, looking at Bryan in his robe.

"It wouldn't work," Bryan said. "They would know you don't belong, and I'm a heretic."

Andi looked through the one-way glass into her interrogation room. After a few seconds, she grabbed Vance and pulled him closer to Bryan. "I've got a plan."

CHAPTER 41

THE PLAN

"So, what's your plan?" Vance asked.

"I'll crack the code on that lock and open the door. When the guard comes in to investigate, we'll clobber him," Andi said matter-of-factly.

"Hold on," Vance said. "You don't know how many guards are out there, or whether they have guns. And you don't know where we're going if we even get out."

"Our priority is to warn Belfore that this cult is going to blow up the induction coil. We've got to notify someone."

"There's a terminal in the backup control room," Bryan said. "We might be able to hack through the firewall and send a message."

"How far?" Andi asked.

"It's just down the corridor, right outside the communion hall."

"What about the guards?" Vance asked. "And everyone else around here?"

"It's almost time for afternoon mass. Attendance is mandatory."

"Everyone goes?" Andi asked.

"They'll leave one guard, maybe two, but the rest of the compound will be empty."

"Where do they go?" Vance asked.

"The communion hall."

"Where the induction coil is?"

Bryan nodded.

Vance furrowed his eyebrows. "Didn't you just say the control room is right outside the communion hall?"

"You don't understand," Bryan said. "Everyone's full attention will be on the Prophet."

"Brainwashing maintenance," Andi said. "How long does it last?"

"Thirty minutes," Bryan said.

"Won't there be someone in the control room?" Vance asked.

"It's just a backup. They run everything from the chapel."

Simulated bells chimed through the compound's speaker system.

"That's the call to mass," Bryan said. "It takes about five minutes for everybody to assemble."

"We need to determine how many guards are outside," Andi said.

She went into Vance's interrogation room and tried to look through the crack between the door and the floor.

"There's no gap at the bottom of the door. I can't see anything." She returned to her room and shut the back door. "I need some water," she shouted and put her ear up next to the door. There wasn't a response, but she heard someone shuffling their feet around, so there was at least one guard.

"There's at least one," she said when she returned to Bryan and Vance. "We need to get those lights off. I want them blind when they enter the room."

"And how are we going to do that?" Vance asked.

Andi used a chair to get on top of the table. She reached up, but she was several feet short of reaching the florescent bulbs. She looked down at Vance. "You'll have to boost me up."

"I can't lift you up that high," he said.

"I'm going to stand on your shoulders."

Vance reluctantly climbed up on the table.

"Squat down," she said.

"What?" Vance said.

"Just do it," Andi said and took off her shoes. "I've done this a hundred times."

She was a cheerleader in high school, so it wasn't a big deal for her to get up on someone's shoulders. Once upon a time, she wanted to be a gymnast, but the mindless repetition of training couldn't compete with the dynamics of acting. Cheerleading was a way for her to taste acrobatics without making a long-term commitment. The experience had honed her balance and taught her to suppress the fear of falling. Vance, whose shoulders she was standing on, didn't have the same level of confidence. It didn't help that their first attempt was on top of a table.

He squatted down, she climbed up on his shoulders, and he shakily stood while grasping her feet. At her new height, she easily reached the light fixture. She twisted one of the four-foot-long bulbs until it came loose. The room dimmed, and she handed the glass tube down to Bryan.

"We might need these later," she said.

She removed the second bulb and handed it down. Vance shuffled over to the other side of the table under the second light fixture, and Andi loosened the first bulb plunging the room into darkness. With no visual cues, Vance started to sway back and forth.

"Let go of my legs," Andi said.

Vance hesitated but complied as his oscillations became more profound.

She jumped back and dropped, clasping onto Vance to slow her descent. There was a thud when she landed on the table.

After a tense moment waiting to see if the guards would rush in to investigate, the three relaxed.

"I've never done a dismount like that in the dark," she said.

Bryan, with the two bulbs in his hands, opened the back door to let in some light. It wasn't much, but they placed the chairs on their sides in an arrangement that would trip anyone who entered.

"I'm going work on the lock's code," Andi said.

Bryan closed the back door, and the three made their way in the darkness to the keypad by the front door. Vance tripped on a chair, and it banged into another. All three froze, but the guard didn't react.

Once in position, Andi queued up the audio recording of the lock being opened when Moody came in earlier. All she had was the sound of the button presses, but she had it in stereo, and she had precise timing information. She knew it was five digits, and one repeated. After playing through the tracks in her mind several times, she started to visualize a pattern. She could see the durations between the presses. Longer gaps meant the button presses were farther apart. She had left and right tracks and used them to perceive horizontal motion. Discerning the vertical motion was more difficult, but she reduced the combinations by factoring in the latency between the presses. There was no starting point, so she would try the pattern starting at different locations until it worked. She ran her fingers over the keypad in the darkness and mimicked the pattern she had in her mind, but didn't press the buttons.

After a few dozen practice rounds, she said, "I'm ready."

"Are you sure?" Vance asked.

"Yes, but it may take me a few tries," Andi said and started entering codes.

A red light flashed at the top of the keypad, and an annoying beep sounded after each try.

"Back away from the door," the guard said from the other side.

"I got their attention," Andi whispered and tried another variation of the code.

"Step away from the door."

"I know this is the right code, it has to be," she said and entered it again. The red light flashed.

"Step away from the door," the guard yelled.

"You're definitely getting his attention," Vance whispered.

"Good grief," she said. "I didn't flip the pattern around. The keypad on the outside is facing the opposite direction. She entered a new code, and a green light flashed. The mechanical bolt hummed, and the door popped open a few inches.

The three captives crouched behind the opening door, shielding themselves from whoever rushed in.

They waited for several seconds, but nothing happened.

Then the door burst open and slammed all three of them against the wall behind it.

One guard stumbled over a chair and fell to the ground. Andi stepped out from her hiding place and shoved the other guard toward the chairs causing him to fall as well. The three ran out the door and slammed it shut behind them.

"Stop right there!" a third guard shouted. He was waiting outside, and he had a Taser drawn on them.

Andi didn't even think. She grabbed one of the fluorescent bulbs Bryan was still holding onto and swung it like a sword as hard as she could. It struck the man's head. The bulb shattered spraying tiny bits of glass and phosphorous coating on his face. He yelped and reached up for his eyes. Bryan wrenched the Taser out of his hand and fired the tiny electrodes into his chest. The guard dropped to the floor and convulsed to the rhythm of the clicking sound made by the weapon. When Bryan released the trigger, the guard passed out.

"Bryan!" Andi said, astonished by his action.

"I had to make sure he didn't set off the alarm," he said. "I told you. I'm getting you out of here."

They heard chairs banging around inside the interrogation room.

"We need to get away from here," Vance said. "Right now."

Bryan motioned them to follow, and they ran down the corridor.

CHAPTER 42

THE SACRIFICE

Andi, Bryan, and Vance raced down the corridor. Their destination was just outside the communion hall where Moody had gathered his whole congregation. His voice boomed louder as the three approached. Andi couldn't understand all his pontificating, but the Prophet would say something, and his crowd chanted back a pre-programmed response. Into the lion's den, she thought as they got closer. But they had to warn Belfore about its imminent annihilation, and the computer in the backup control room was their best prospect.

"I hope they didn't change the code," Bryan whispered when they reached a nondescript door at the end of the corridor.

"What?" Vance said, straining to keep his volume down. "You should have mentioned that was a possibility."

Bryan entered the code, and nothing happened.

Andi's heart sank.

He entered it again. After a seemingly infinite pause, a green light flashed followed by a click. The three hurried into the room and gently shut the door.

The control room was an oversized closet with a single chair and a console. A bank of video monitors lined the narrow wall and showed views of the communion hall and the staging area.

"This is it?" Andi asked. "I was expecting something more extravagant, like everything else around here."

"The chapel is where most operations take place," Bryan said. "They only use this room when there's a problem with the main system."

"How long until they look in here?" Vance asked.

"They won't look in here," Bryan said. "This console is rarely used, and most people don't even know about it."

"Yeah," Vance said. "But they're all just outside the door."

Bryan studied the console. "It looks like they are charging the induction coil. It's almost reached the portal threshold."

"They're getting it ready to drop all three of us in the Void," Vance said.

"I don't think so," Andi said. "They're going to see if they can reproduce the exit portal I discovered."

"What?" Bryan and Vance said in unison. Their mouths remained open.

"Oh, that's right. You two were out of the loop." She tilted her head back. "I discovered an exit portal inside the Void. Well, I accidentally discovered it."

"And you're just now telling us this?" Vance asked. His tone was sharp.

"Since I used that secret to stop your execution, the appropriate response was: Thank you for saving my life," Andi said.

"Thank you for saving my life," Vance repeated. "Can you please tell us about what you found?"

"I, Andalusia Fyffe, have discovered a practical use for the Void." She wobbled her head. "Nobody would have even entertained the idea that an actor, a failing student, would be the one to crack open the Void's deepest secret. I believed Voidology was the world's biggest waste of time, a sham, a con, a game of three-card monte, a useless drain of resources. I thought you two were mindless cogs in the giant, academic welfare-machine we lovingly refer to as the grant. Even after being thrown out of the prog—"

"Dude," Vance interrupted. "Get on with it."

"Oh, all right," she said in an annoyed tone. "Remember how the woman showed us the inside of the lunch box before sending me into the Void," she said to Vance.

"The power supply," Vance said.

"And inside the box was a miniature induction coil that you said was too small to open a portal."

Vance nodded.

"But it did open a portal," she said, "and it leads to the outside. Can you believe that?"

"What do you mean by *outside*?" Vance asked. "Outside the Void?"

Andi made an exaggerated nod. "When they dropped me into the Void, I was so super focused on listening to the resonator hum that I wasn't paying attention when the container stopped moving. I bounced around, and the power supply came off its hook. It hit the side and popped open. But the little ring," she said and made a circular shape with her index fingers and thumbs. "It wasn't in there." She pulled her hands apart a few inches to frame the diagonal corners of a rectangle. "The power supply box filled with a view of the outside, like really outside. I saw trees and sky."

Vance and Bryan stared at Andi in disbelief.

"When they pulled me out, I saw the ground flying by through the box. It was moving by so fast I couldn't make out anything, but it looked like the ground whizzing by. The outside view faded right before I exited the Void."

"That's incredible," Bryan said. "The power supply is one of the Church's most advanced inventions, but it requires the mesh shielding to function in the Void."

"Maybe it needed to be a certain distance from the interference generated by the larger induction coil before this effect happens," Vance added.

"How far did they stick me in the Void?" Andi asked.

"The pole assembly can only extend twenty-five feet after the chamber seal engages," Bryan said.

"I was miles away and looking into a forest."

"We drove through trees when we came here," Vance said. "It's more likely that you saw the outside of this compound."

"It was a lot farther away than that," Andi said. "You didn't see how fast everything moved by in the box."

Vance scratched his beard.

"But how did I move across the ground? They inserted the capsule straight down into the Void?" she asked.

"The twins have a theory suggesting the Void is an extra-dimensional layer, a thin sheet of space-time, balanced between the mass differential around the planet. You would always travel horizontally across the ground since it doesn't have depth as we perceive it."

Andi shrugged. "If you say so."

"We don't know if you actually saw a portal," Vance said. "It could just be an image of the outside." He paused before continuing. "It may have been a hallucination. You were under some heavy-duty stress."

"Jeez, I know what I saw, and it was definitely a portal," Andi said. "When I reached through it, a pine needle got stuck on my sleeve, and that's what convinced Moody."

"Do you know how dangerous that was?" Vance's tone was a mix of astonishment and scolding. "It could have torn your arm off, and you would've bled to death before they pulled you out of the Void. It could have sucked you through like Jonathan Rutledge and his assistant. There are so many ways that could have gone wrong."

Andi crossed her arms. "If I hadn't reached through it, we wouldn't know for sure it was an exit."

"True," Vance said, "but it was still reckless."

"I didn't know you cared," she said, "but I didn't lose my arm."

"How did you fit your arm through the miniature ring?"

Andi grimaced. "You weren't listening. The exit portal wasn't limited to the center of the ring like a regular portal. It filled the entire box, and I couldn't even see the ring."

"Maybe it's projected in front of the ring, and the shielding around the box limited its size," Vance said. "We need to take the ring out of the box."

Bryan furrowed his brows. "Outside the box, an exit might expand to the wall of the immersion capsule. It also has shielding properties."

"And that would be large enough for a person to pass through," Vance said.

"Sure thing," Andi said. "I'll try taking the ring out next time."

"We need to run some tests and define what the limit is," Bryan said. "This could be a new field of study."

"Are you sure they don't know about this here?" Vance asked.

Bryan shook his head. "As far as anyone knows, an unshielded power supply becomes inert in the Void."

"I wish I could take some of those mini-rings with us," Vance said. His excitement belied their dire situation. "We could use the test pod for my propulsion tests and navigate using your portal tracking system. Can you program Belfore's fabricator to reproduce the shielding mesh?"

"I think so," Bryan said. "It's just a minor variation of the one I used in my portal location test."

Andi cleared her throat to get their attention. "We kind of have more pressing issues here than your dissertations."

Bryan turned to the console and typed in some commands. He tried accessing email and messaging, but they were all locked out. He tried searching for unprotected ports in the firewall, but the Church's security was solid. His expression twisted the more he failed. "I can't get a message out from this computer."

"Keep trying," Andi said.

"Mass is almost over," he said and switched the camera view of the communion hall to a larger screen, and they watched the round room empty.

A minute later a speaker in the backup control room clicked a few times, and Moody's voice blared above their heads.

"There is no way to escape the compound, Miss Fyffe. Surrender immediately, or my research will proceed without you."

Andi turned to Bryan. "Your father's nuts." She twirled her finger next to her head.

Vance sighed. "He'll never let us go. It won't matter how many times he sends you into the Void."

Bryan shook his head. "He won't. The Church will never allow the possibility of their work being exposed."

"This may sound crazy," Vance said, "but what if we all three squeeze into that immersion capsule, drop it in the Void, and get out through one of Andi's exit portals?"

"You're right. That's crazy," Andi said. "More like suicide."

"You're the one who's so sure it's an exit," Vance said. "Do you have a better idea?"

Andi shook her head. "What happened to all that caution you were throwing at us earlier?"

"What do you think they'll do to us when they find us?" Vance asked.

Andi didn't say anything.

Bryan keyed more commands into the console. "By the time we make it to the immersion capsule, the coil will be fully charged." He slid a device out of its charging station and held it up. "This remote well let me operate the coil from the staging area."

"Can we get there without being seen?" Andi asked.

"The elevator's just fifty feet away," Bryan said and flipped a switch. The video monitor changed to show the corridors outside the control room and a robed man walking by.

"Won't that be the first place they'll look?" Vance asked.

Andi smiled. "No, they think we're trying to get out the front door. They'll never expect us to escape through the Void."

The corridor cleared, and the three made their way to the elevator and rode up to the staging room's level. When the doors slid open, a robed woman waited for them.

"Good grief," Andi said.

It was the attendant from her previous trips into the Void, but her face showed no sign of anything wrong. She pulled up her hood and moved out of the way so the three could exit the elevator. She then boarded and pushed a button. As the doors slid shut, she smiled at Bryan.

Vance clenched his fists. "She's getting the others."

Bryan shook his head. "No, she won't."

"What makes you think that?" Andi asked.

"Because she's my mother, and she would never put me in danger even if it meant defying the Prophet."

"Other than raise you in a cult," Andi said and paused. "Sorry, I shouldn't have been so blunt."

A row of lockers along the staging area's wall contained dozens of protective suits, power supplies, and air canisters. Andi and Bryan put their equipment on first, then helped Vance with his many flaps and buckles. Bryan motioned to a sliding switch on his suit's hood, and all three turned on their built-in communications system.

"Testing. One. Two. Three," he said.

"I hear you loud and clear," Vance said.

Andi nodded. "Me too."

Bryan used the remote to unpark the immersion capsule from its ceiling hideaway. It required the specialized tool to unlock the clamshell door.

"Do we really want to do this?" Andi asked through her suit's com.

Before Bryan and Vance responded, a speaker above their heads clicked to life. It was Moody, again.

"Miss Fyffe, your time has elapsed. The Church has a method for dealing with heretics. Prepare yourself for a final communion."

"I guess we have nothing to lose," she said and got into the capsule.

Vance followed, but Bryan didn't.

"Come on!" Andi motioned to speed him up.

"You can't latch the door from the inside. You have to go without me."

"Wait a minute," Vance said. "We're all getting out of here."

"If you don't go, my father will destroy Belfore and kill everyone there."

"But you can't stay here," Andi said. "You'll die."

"You are the only ones who can stop the Church from overloading the ring," Bryan said. "I have to stay here and make sure you get the chance."

"Then why did you put on the suit?" Andi asked.

"I needed the com-system to talk to you, and I didn't want you to ask a bunch of questions and delay your departure." Bryan handed Vance an extra power source. "Use this one to open the exit portal." He sealed the capsule and primed the immersion sequence.

Andi looked into Vance's faceplate. "You realize this may just dump us out into the Void, and we'll die a horrible, painful death."

"At least Moody won't get the satisfaction of doing it himself," Vance said.

"True," she said.

"Have some faith, Andi." Bryan pushed a button, sending the capsule down to the platform in the communion hall.

CHAPTER 43

THE ENTRY

The communion hall was empty when Andi and Vance started their descent from the ceiling. By the time the capsule reached the chamber containing the induction coil, a contingency of white-uniformed guards had surrounded them. They aimed assault rifles at them, but Bryan had already started the automated procedure.

The container and its passengers dropped through a hatch and into the chamber. The seal deployed around the insertion pole, and pumps evacuated the air. Pastel colors flickered below Andi and Vance's feet until the portal flashed open. The guards lowered their rifles. If they damaged the chamber now, the open portal could suck them all into the Void.

"Good luck," Bryan said over the com.

Andi and Vance heard a commotion before his com went dead. They assumed Moody's men had gotten to him. Andi hoped his father wasn't crazy enough to kill his own son, but she didn't know.

The telescoping pole pushed the immersion capsule into the Void. It was Andi's third trip. She felt like a pro as she braced for the change in gravity. Vance was awestruck and floated until he bumped his head on the top of the capsule. He gazed up at the light from the open portal as it shrank away.

Andi pried on the access panel of the extra power supply with her fingers, but she couldn't get it open. The protective suit's thick gloves made it too difficult for her to unlatch the panel door.

"Hey, I need some help here," she said but didn't get a response. "Vance!" she yelled, but still no response. The com system no longer functioned inside the Void. The capsule was still filled with air, but there was too much noise absorbing material between them. She leaned over and pressed her faceplate up against his. "I can't get the box open."

Vance didn't respond.

"Can you hear me!"

"I'm going to be sick." He was gasping for air.

"Don't stare at the light from the portal. Close your eyes and take slow, deep breaths. The motion sickness will pass." She heard his breathing slow.

"It's space sickness, not motion sickness."

"Whatever," Andi said. "I can't get the box open."

Vance pried on the box, but it took them both to get the panel off.

Light filled the capsule, and they shielded their eyes against the brightness and watched a blur of colors whiz by.

"It took us too long to get the box open. The portal is already open," she said.

"I think we have a problem," Vance said, sounding less green.

Andi reached into the box, but her hand went through to the other side. All she felt was the wind whipping by, almost pulling her in, but there was no ring to grab. Her heart dropped. She pressed her faceplate against Vance's. "I'll try to get the ring out of the box."

"How?" he asked but didn't get a reply.

Andi's preconception of gravity compelled her to maneuver around in the weightlessness so she could place the box against the floor of the capsule. She felt idiotic after wasting time to reorient herself when there wasn't any gravity to dictate which end was the floor.

She swung the box back and slammed it into the floor of the capsule. Her hope was to dislodge the ring, but the force of her swing propelled her in the opposite direction. Vance braced himself against the sides with his feet and held onto Andi so she would remain in place. She tried again and again, but nothing happened. On her final swing, the light in the box flickered out and plunged them into darkness. The exit portal vanished. She reached into the box, but the ring had fallen out.

She tapped on Vance's leg, and he flipped around so they could put their facemasks together.

"It's not in the box, and I can't find it in the dark," she said.

"Keep searching. We've got to get it turned back on."

The capsule insertion reached its apex and jerked to a stop. When Andi and Vance reached out to cancel their momentum, there was a metallic thunk as the floating ring smacked against the floor. It gave off a brief flash of light as the exit tried to reopen. They frantically searched the darkness for the device, but all they did was bump into each other and rebounded off the walls. Andi pressed her faceplate on Vance's.

"We're never going to find it," she said.

"At least I got to be inside the Void," Vance said.

"There goes my Nobel Prize," Andi joked.

Vance laughed.

The capsule jerked again and started its journey back out of the Void. Vance reached out to grab the sides, and Andi held onto him.

"Moody must have overridden the cycle because we haven't been in long enough," she said.

"I don't know why he's bothering to pull us out. He just going to stick us back in."

A clink against Andi's faceplate startled her. She raked her hands through the darkness, trying to grab the ring, but she only knocked it out of reach. It slapped against the floor, and a bright light exploded out of the donut sized ring. An exit portal appeared with the same circumference as the capsule. Before the two could react, gravity from the other side yanked them through the doorway.

CHAPTER 44

THE EXIT

The exit portal spat Andi and Vance out of the Void ten feet above the forest floor. Their exit vector luckily missed any trees head-on, and the wire weave of their suits deflected the spear-like branches that would have otherwise punctured their bodies. They landed in a thick layer of pine needles, and the two were still holding onto each other when they came to a rest. Andi wanted to lie there for a minute and make sure her bones were all in one piece, but Vance started convulsing and clawed at his faceplate.

She sprang into action and unlatched his mask. He struggled to breathe but sucked in a breath of fresh air.

"Are you okay?" she asked, but he couldn't hear her. She ripped off her faceplate and repeated the question.

Vance labored to breathe but managed a nod.

"I don't know how much time we have, where we are, or which way we need to go," she said, "but we've got to get a move on."

Vance had recovered enough to talk. "Pick a direction," he gasped. "I'll follow."

She helped him up, and they started moving through the trees.

After a twenty-minute hike through the forest, they came upon a dirt road. After ten more minutes, they reached a paved, two-lane highway. Three cars passed them before a beat-up truck pulled off the road in front of them. The driver was a white-haired man with a bushy beard. Two floppy-eared bloodhounds sat next to him on the bench seat with their tongues hanging out.

"Aren't you two a little far from the water?" he asked.

Andi didn't know what he was talking about until she realized they were still wearing the protective suits.

"We have an emergency. Do you have a cell phone?" she asked.

"No, ma'am," he said. "Never owned one."

"We've got to call the police or the FBI. It's life or death. Can you take us to a phone?"

"Sure thing, but you'll have to hop in the back." He motioned to the truck bed.

"How far are we from Belfore?"

"Where?" he asked in an uncertain tone.

"Belfore University."

"Oh. Right. That's a couple of states away." He laughed. "Go Bulls!"

"Horns up," she said in a flat tone accompanied by the hand gesture response. She looked at Vance and then back at the driver. "Where exactly are we?"

"You, little lady, are southwest of Bowling Green in the great Commonwealth of Kentucky. Just how lost are you two?"

"Good grief," Andi said. She unhooked her power supply and plunked it in the back of the truck.

"Be careful with that," Vance said. "We may not get any more." He cradled the power supply attached to his suit.

"I can tell you where there's a locker full of them," she said.

"Well," Vance said and grinned. "You're back on track for that Nobel Prize in physics."

"If everyone at Belfore dies, there won't be much joy in that."

A few minutes later, the driver dropped them off at a gas station.

"A pay phone," Andi said. "How quaint."

She dialed 911, but it was a waste of time. She couldn't convince the local authorities in backwoods Kentucky that a cult was about to blow up a second-rate college in another state.

"They hung up on me," she said with a confused expression.

Next, she tried to call her father, but she had never made a collect call and had to ask Vance what to do. She got an operator to make the call, but Dean Fyffe didn't answer, and she couldn't leave a message since nobody accepted the charges. She redialed the operator and asked to be connected with the FBI's emergency number. Five transfers later she was able to tell someone that the Rutties were about to blow up Belfore. When she told them that Special Agent Michael Hayden was working for the bad guys, they stopped believing her.

Andi then called the Belfore campus police.

"Campus Dispatch, what's your emergency?" a gruff voice said.

"This is Andalusia Fyffe, my father's the dean of physics. There's a crazy cult trying to overload the induction coil in the physics building. It's going to explode and blow up the entire campus."

"Where are you calling from?" His voice was skeptical.

"It doesn't matter where I am. You've got to get everyone to evacuate the whole campus. I don't know how much time is left."

"The FBI has already been here. If there were a problem, they would have taken care of it."

"The FBI has people in on it. Special Agent Michael Hayden kidnapped us and killed our professors. He's working with the cult."

"Is this a prank, ma'am? You'll be charged with a misdemeanor."

She let out a frustrated sigh. "Why won't you listen to me? I'm one of those students the FBI is supposed to be protecting, except they tried to kill me." She paused to calm down. "You're missing the point of this phone call. There is going to be an explosion, and you've got to get everyone off campus. Right now!"

"It's a serious crime to make a false bomb threat. That's a felony."

Andi shrieked with frustration. "You will be one of those people who dies when the ring overloads."

"Are you threatening a police officer, ma'am?"

Andi handed Vance the phone. "You tell them," she ordered.

"This is Vance McMullen. Everything Andi just told you is the truth. There's a group of people dressed as lab techs—they may even be techs—who are going to attach a device to the induction coil in the physics building. It will cause a very large explosion. You need to get everyone evacuated."

"Everyone in the physics building?"

"Everyone on the campus," he said. "And get someone to cut the power to the induction coil. They can't overload it without external power."

"Are you two working on this prank together? You'll both be charged with a crime."

Vance told Andi what the officer said, and she snatched the phone out of his hand and hung it up. "What's with these people? Why won't anyone take us seriously?"

Andi's last call was to the dean's office. The receptionist, Mary, accepted the collect call.

"Mary, I'm so glad I got through to you. I've got to talk to my father. It's really urgent."

"Andi, he's been with the FBI all day trying to find out where they took you," she said. "Where are you?"

"Vance and I are in Kentucky. Long story. No time. That cult is going to blow up the induction coil in the physics building. You've got to get off campus and get everyone else to evacuate. We called the campus police, but they didn't believe us."

"Blow up the physics building?"

"Yes, the one you're currently in."

"Okay, Andi," Mary said, taking Andi at her word. "I have my purse in hand and am heading out the door. Goodbye."

The call ended.

"At least she believed us." Andi hung up the phone. "So, what do we do now?"

"There's nothing else we can do."

"How are we going to get back to Belfore?"

Vance shrugged.

"And where can I get something else to wear?"

He laughed. "We do look pretty ridiculous."

"What about Bryan?" She frowned.

Vance didn't know how to respond.

Ten minutes later, the pay phone rang. Andi picked it up, and the sound of her father's voice surprised her. Mary had written down the number from her caller ID and passed it along to the dean. She had also pulled the fire alarm and evacuated the physics building. Mary deserved a raise.

Mary had also contacted the campus police and confirmed everything Andi had told them. They apprehended five members of the cult who had already attached a smaller induction coil to Belfore's one-meter ring and were trying to energize both when the power to the building shut off.

The Bowling Green Police Department dispatched a car to take Andi and Vance to the airport, after stopping off at a Walmart to buy them some clothes. A new FBI team met them at the airport and escorted them the rest of the way back to Belfore. Andi and Vance remained in protective custody for a few days, but the FBI put them in a hotel instead of the dormitory. It wasn't a four-star, but it was the best Belfore had to offer.

CHAPTER 45

THE COGITATION

Andi appreciated her second round of sequestration. Being protected in a nice hotel had more perks than it did in a crappy dormitory. She had access to a gym and pool. There was a spa, and she could order as much room service as she wanted. There was even a vegan menu. More importantly, she had time to process how a cult and the Void turned her world upside down.

Her acting career was over. More precisely, it had never begun. She didn't even seem to care about that anymore. She still wanted to be an actor, but she no longer cared what the director, David, thought about her. That simple paradigm shift was liberating, and she liked it.

Not so long ago, she believed Voidology was a fraud and the laughingstock of the scientific community, but her views had evolved. She had done more—intentionally or not—to advance the science than anyone. She even took a little pride in that, and there was certainly no lack of irony. After the FBI cleaned up the cult mess, she was going to demand that her father let her back into the Voidology program, even if she had to pay for it herself.

The twins had already solved their Void modeling equations using the information Andi brought back from her first trip into the Void. The new data she gathered on her second trip using Moody's modified resonator was a windfall and would keep the kids busy for years. They were well on their way to becoming the youngest recipients of the Nobel Prize. Andi didn't know if she would get any credit, but she didn't care. She was thrilled for Vernon and Helena, and she wasn't going to end up like Daniel Moody chasing after credit his whole life.

Sequestration also gave Andi time to think about Bryan. She thought he was her friend, but he betrayed her. Then he risked everything to save her and Vance. Without his help, they wouldn't have escaped from the cult's compound, and the Rutties would have destroyed Belfore. She had conflicts to resolve and still didn't know how to feel about Bryan, but she wouldn't write him off.

Her former enemy, Vance, was now her best friend. They shared a death-defying experience together and were the first ones to traverse the Void. It had brought them a lot closer than she could acknowledge. She didn't know how to feel about that either, but she was going to see where it led.

CHAPTER 46

THE TAKEDOWN

Two days after Andi and Vance returned to Belfore, the FBI raided the Church's compound. Of the three-hundred-member congregation, most surrendered immediately and wanted to get out. Moody had abducted or blackmailed much of his congregation. Others joined to find God but were shaken by the Church's extreme methods. A few were loyal to the Prophet all the way to the end, but they didn't put up a fight.

The security guards and other hired help were not as eager to surrender, but they were accustomed to dealing with brainwashed cult members. They were no match for well-trained agents on an equal footing. The FBI takedown was swift and decisive.

Andi and Vance both briefed the FBI on how Bryan had helped them escape and stressed to them that Belfore would no longer exist without his help. They found him locked in one of the interrogation rooms with a broken arm and a badly bruised face, but he was alive.

Daniel Moody and Jason Reed weren't present when the FBI descended upon the compound. They had conveniently left after the immersion capsule returned from the Void without its occupants or any sign of their exit. Millions of dollars had been transferred out of the cult's front business, and the Church's private jet was missing.

Most of those rescued by the FBI were too afraid to speculate where the Prophet might have gone, but Bryan wasn't. He was also familiar with his father's getaways and helped narrow down his location. Three days later, the FBI arrested Moody and Reed playing blackjack at a Las Vegas casino.

CHAPTER 47

THE DEBUT

A year later, Belfore was finishing its spring midterms. The Voidology department had grown to twenty-five students and added seven new faculty members. Between Andi's discoveries and the twins completing their mathematical model of the Void's topology, Belfore had never been more popular. The university was once again the shiny new thing. There were even rumors of the grant being expanded.

Andi stayed in the Voidology program and enjoyed presenting the weekly exhibition more than she ever thought possible. She was also a celebrity, at least in scientific circles, and the auditorium was packed every week. Reservations were required. She was, after all, responsible for the biggest breakthrough since the Void's discovery and had become one of the most knowledgeable people in the field.

The Dark Crowd Players dissolved after David's breakdown, so Andi started her own theater group. Her newfound celebrity status translated from the scientific community all the way down to the local theater, and she didn't mind capitalizing on it to pursue her dream of being an actor. She had invited all the Dark Crowd Players to join her, and most did. Their first performance was *Macbeth*, and it was opening night. She played Lady Macbeth and was a little nervous. Even after surviving cult kidnappings and being dropped repeatedly into the Void, she still had butterflies. She sat in front of a lighted mirror and made some minor adjustments to her makeup. She closed her eyes and ran through her meditation drills. It worked until the door clicked open and startled her. She tried to turn around and see who it was, but her bulky dress wouldn't allow it.

"Hello." Her voice almost trembled, and she reached for a pair of scissors sticking out of her makeup case.

"Andi," Vance said.

"Oh my god." Her insides relax. "I thought you were someone else." She laughed and discreetly put the scissors down on the vanity before he saw them.

"I have a surprise for you," he said. "Make that two surprises."

Andi carefully stood, fluffed her long flowing dress, and turned around. Vance held out a bouquet of red roses. Andi smiled ear to ear, but the roses were only part of the surprise. Bryan was there too.

"Bryan!" She ran over to give him a hug. She hadn't seen him in several months. He'd been recovering, physically and mentally. "I'm so glad to see you."

"I couldn't miss opening night," Bryan said.

"Don't I get a hug too?" Vance said.

Andi put her arms around him and gave him a kiss. Then she took the roses. "They're beautiful."

"Stand right there," he said and took her picture with his phone.

Andi leaned toward Bryan. "You're looking good. I approve of the new hairdo and dapper suit."

"Thanks," he said. "I'm trying to fit in."

"Screw that," Andi said. "Just be yourself."

Bryan grinned, but he didn't look at the floor.

Andi raised her eyebrows. "Are you here to stay?"

"I think so."

"And you'll be back in the Voidology program?"

"If I can get back in," he said. "And find a way to pay for it."

"Don't worry about that." She grinned. "I have some pull with the dean."

EPILOGUE

THE NEXT GENERATION

THIRTY YEARS LATER

Liz ran down the steps to the station as quickly as she could in her long dress and painfully uncomfortable shoes. She glanced at her watch. The scheduled departure was only thirty seconds away, but she hoped there would be a delay. There never was, and the shuttle had already left.

The New York to London transatlantic portal line ran every fifteen minutes, and the extra wait gave her a chance to go through her speech again. Besides, she had thirty minutes before she was supposed to meet Seamus at the Red Lion Pub in Chelsea.

She caught the next shuttle and made it to the pub with ten minutes to spare.

"Liz!" a red-headed man wearing a tuxedo hollered from the bar. He held up a pint and waved her over.

The place was packed, and Liz carefully navigated her way through the crowd. It was bad enough that she had to wear a dress, but she didn't want beer spilled on it before she even made it to the awards ceremony.

"Hey, you look stunning," Seamus said and handed her a fresh pint.

"You clean up pretty well yourself." Liz took a sip of the dark beer, hoping the alcohol would stop her feet from hurting but not so much as to make her forget her speech.

"It's not every day my fiancée gets the Isaac Newton Medal."

"Medal?" the barman said.

"Liz, here, is getting one of the most prestigious awards in the country." Seamus held up his glass. "To Liz," he shouted.

"To Liz!" Everyone else in the bar shouted in reply and took a drink.

"You're embarrassing me," she said in a quiet tone. "They're just giving me the medal because my grandfather discovered the Void."

"Are you kidding me?" he said. "You single-handedly figured out how to squeeze energy out of the Void and solved the world's energy crisis. The King should be here buying you a pint."

She waved her hand to dismiss his statement. "I didn't do it alone. Besides, if your mother hadn't finagled me into the program, I wouldn't even have gotten into the field. She should be the one getting this medal."

"Mom doesn't care about awards." Seamus finished his beer with a single gulp. "She gets more out of helping others."

Liz took another sip of her beer and put it back on the bar. "I was late getting here; we should head over to the Institute." She stood and straightened out her dress.

"Congratulations, Miss Rutledge," the barman said.

"Thanks," she said and smiled.

"Bring that medal back here and let us take a gander."

Seamus took Liz's hand and cleared a path for her as they exited the pub. They walked down the street to the closest intra-city hub, where permanent portals connected different points in the city. The Institute of Physics was only one jump away.

"I wish your mom could have been here too," Liz said.

"I do too," Seamus said, "but she didn't want to distract from your night."

"I sometimes forget she's a celebrity."

"Are you nervous about giving your speech?"

She stopped walking and looked at him. "Why would you say that?"

"Because you've been clutching that rolled up note card like it's the Great Star of Africa."

Liz pressed her lips together and stared at Seamus. "We don't all have one of those handy-dandy recorders built into our brains."

He snorted. "You don't need it. You'll be the smartest person in the building tonight, and everyone there will be in awe." He wobbled his head, just like his mother did when she knew she was right.

"That's doesn't help me give a speech." She frowned.

"Just start talking about the quantum-fold extraction technique you came up with. You'll mesmerize them."

Liz smiled and relaxed her grip on the notecard.

The two entered an arched doorway and emerged across town at King's Cross Station. The transition was seamless and no different from walking through a doorway into another room. The Institute of Physics was two blocks away, and they headed toward the station's exit.

"Seamus! Liz!" A short guy in a tuxedo shouted from across the station. He ran toward them, almost knocking down several other travelers.

"Dude, what's the hurry?" Seamus asked.

"You have to come and see what I discovered," he said out of breath.

"What is it, B.J.?" Liz asked as she gripped her notes a little tighter.

"I found something with the new scanners. You won't believe it. It's incredible. I triple-checked everything before I came. You've got to see it."

"We're on our way to the Institute," Seamus said.

"I found a filament." B.J. paused to catch his breath. "I sent a pulse through it, and the echo didn't return for 500 nanoseconds."

"What do you mean, 500 nanoseconds?" Liz wrinkled her brow as she ran through the computations in her head. "That would have to travel over 200,000 miles one way."

"Exactly," B.J. said, nodding furiously. "And what's 200,000 miles away?"

"The Moon." Liz let the word hang in the air while she and Seamus considered the implications.

"Are you saying that the Void reaches all the way to the Moon?" Seamus asked.

"I think the filament connects Earth's Void to another one on the Moon."

"Are there more of these filaments?" Liz asked.

"Yes, but this one was the strongest."

Liz turned to Seamus. "We've got to check this out."

"What about the awards ceremony?" he said.

"It's just a dumb medal."

"You need to go get the dumb medal," Seamus said.

B.J. pulled a flat card out of his coat pocket and brought up the results from his test. "I'll show you the details on the way to the Institute."

"Okay, but I want to go back to Belfore as soon as we're done."

ABOUT THE AUTHOR

Joey Rogers is an enthusiast of sci-fi, video games, and all-around geekery. He's a software developer by day in the high-tech city of Huntsville, Alabama and loves writing about what the future might hold. His other novels are:

A Funny Thing Happened on the Moon
An Alien, a Time Machine, and a Loser
An Alien, a Time Machine, and a Hero

Website: www.gegodyne.com
Twitter: @gegodyne
Email: gegodyne@gmail.com
Facebook: www.facebook.com/gegodyne